T0107295

"FUNNY WATER AND BOB"

by
Jack Risin
SAG

Writers Guild of America, West

Registration 1998, 2004 and 2008

iUniverse, Inc.
New York   Bloomington

FUNNY WATER AND BOB

Copyright © 2009 by J.R. Butcher

All rights reserved. No part of this book may be used
or reproduced by any means, graphic, electronic, or
mechanical, including photocopying, recording, taping or
by any information storage retrieval system without the
written permission of the publisher except in the case of brief
quotations embodied in critical articles and reviews.

iUniverse books may be ordered through booksellers or by contacting:
iUniverse
1663 Liberty Drive
Bloomington, IN 47403
www.iuniverse.com
1-800-Authors (1-800-288-4677)

Because of the dynamic nature of the Internet, any Web addresses or
links contained in this book may have changed since publication and
may no longer be valid. The views expressed in this work are solely those
of the author and do not necessarily reflect the views of the publisher,
and the publisher hereby disclaims any responsibility for them.

ISBN: 978-1-4401-1637-7 (pbk)
ISBN: 978-1-4401-1638-4 (ebk)

Printed in the United States of America

iUniverse rev. date: 01/12/2009

Preface

This story was written in 1988/89 and in 1991, after buying a used Bronco, I drove to the gold country area and encountered the valley, the 1955 bridge, and the meadow, hence adding the Bronco and real valley to my story.

In 1996 as an actor at age 55, I was ask to present my story to an audience of Movie Producers/Directors, TV Directors, Editors and actors in the form of a "Treatment" for a possible movie. Seven of us presented our stories or "Treatments" as they are called in the movie industry. Not formally understanding what a "Treatment" was I drafted an outline for my presentation and verbally told the story.

After all of our stories were presented and discussed the leading Director, President of Columbia College (CA), Emmy and Oscar winner Bri Murphy, ASC, DGA came up to me at point blank range and said, "Do it, just do it." Not totally comprehending her directness I asked, "What do you mean?" to which she replied, "Do it, it's a real treatment with all the necessary components for a good movie." Over the following months and years I learned about the amazing life of the talented Bri Murphy (more on her below) and joined many others in hoping her life story would someday be a movie.

At this point I dedicated my future to making "Funny Water and Bob" a movie. In doing so I learned the easiest way to over come some of the liabilities that face Producers, Directors, Agents and help them and the many others in the acting world is to put my story into a book.

"Funny Water and Bob" is designed to be a recurring annual movie classic, such as Christmas classics, for the loving people of the Easter season of any religion or culture.

Special Thanks And
Acknowledgements

I have to pass on sincere thanks to some of the people that have encouraged me to write the story, write the treatment and now write the book and help me write and re-write the book. Everyone is blessed with friends that give their verbal encouragements but only a few stand behind their words and sincerely help when needed. I've been blessed with a hand full of great ones. My first wife of 32 years who, until her passing stood by me and some of my strange ideas, Gloria Jean Butcher and my children Jack II and Charlotte Jean Giacoma. My second wife who endures me now, Marilyn E. Butcher.

Director, President of Columbia College, Emmy & Oscar winner, Director of Photography, first woman in the The American Society of Cinematographers and the IATSE, Bri Murphy, ASC, DGA, Emeritus, who saw a new student of the acting craft well into his 50's as a actor/producer/writer and showed her belief in me and had me work on productions with her and her sister.

Rebecca Scaglione, author and writer of a trilogy that I hope to be able to pass on my support in helping her books to become a TV series, encouraged and helping me with the direction of the re-writing and publishing process.

Andrea Spirtos, who selfishly took time out of her life and did the re-writing, the Ghost Writing, the adding/changing of words that made the book flow with style. There must be more that I could say about her but I lack the ability to find the words to describe what it felt like to see and read how she took my words and made them into enhanced sentences that made me want to read the paragraphs over and over. I'm kind of like Big Mamma in the book, I talk in short sentences that mean a lot and hold lots of meanings she made them flow with dignity. I'm very lucky and thankful for knowing her.

Prologue

Easter has always been a time for the little kids to find that special egg, the one left by the Easter Bunny, hidden so as to make finding the egg half the reward. Every year the Ebner family hosts a citywide egg hunt for the kids where it is known that blacks, whites, greens, browns and little grays from Mars can hunt for these special eggs and win prizes.

Vallivue Falls is a small community of about 90,000, forty miles away from the larger cities and has a reputation for being rather quaint. Most of the residents have lived there, or their families have, all of their lives so everyone knows everyone. People grow up here, work here and leave only to go on vacations or visit other relatives. Why leave when we have all the stores, businesses and food that anyone would ever need or want right here, is a common sentiment.

Roberta (Bob) Ebner ventures out of the community after that special Easter egg hunt and finds a prize for everyone to remember, some more than others. Outsiders came to claim the prize that is not theirs. Some resorted to kidnapping members of the family.

What they didn't know is Vallivue Falls is a united idyllic community with love for all that give love. Oh what a price these kidnappers pay.

Nom de plume

Jack Risin

1.

The Park

The couple on the park bench hardly notice the dusk settling over them. The peaceful scene dotted with yellow daffodils and heavy elms trees is interrupted only by the commotion of the heavy lawn equipment being loaded in the bed of the truck parked across the lawn behind them. The air is thick with the aroma of newly mown grass.

Engrossed only with each other, they fail to notice the rusty green van as it pulls between them and the mowing crew. Before they have an opportunity to react, the van door slides open. Three men, each with black hoods, appear with guns drawn and nasty attitudes. The men pull the couple inside the van against their will. Petrified the couple, particularly the man, looks for any identifying mark on the three. With only holes large enough for their eyes, it is impossible to guess who they are. There appears to be no tattooing or other marks on their hands.

The struggle is not long lived. Two of the men are much larger than the young couple. Even though the young man is in excellent shape, they are overcome. The young man and woman are no match in terms of strength and stamina as the captors cover their heads with thick black burlap hoods and tie their hands within a matter of seconds. As their worlds become a void, they are unaware that the smallest hooded man ran to the couple's vehicle and tossed an envelope onto the front seat.

The driver of the van seems to be the leader of this hooded gang and gives all the orders. The van drives around and picks up the note-carrier who looks suspicious with his hood pulled to his forehead. "You stupid idiot! Do you want to be recognized?" yells the driver at the note carrier. "Welllll, no, bbbbut since they can't see what's thththe big diffffffrence?" the Ugly stutters as he jumps into the van the sliding door slams shut behind him. The van quickly speeds off without a notice from the mowing crew as if they were in a coma.

2.

The Factory

The old rusty green van pulls up to a factory-warehouse outside of town.

It is apparent this beat up old factory has just been rented by the driver, Al Mooruny, a little sawed-off mob want-to-be from back east with a heavy accent. By this time all have removed their hoods knowing the young couple can't see through the covering that made their world black.

As the van pulls up to the building, a big camouflaged garage door appears where one seemingly was not there a moment ago. Mooruny had done his homework in selecting this spot. The van drives toward the garage door. The small one jumps out of the van and struggles to open the big, heavy door while the other two big burley ones watch and laugh. Finally getting it open, the small one hops back into the vehicle.

The van drives into the warehouse, turns to the left and parks as if it were getting ready to drive back out. The instant the van stops, the Uglys remove the kids and rush to get out, stumbling over each other's feet. "Stupid idiots!" Mooruny mutters under his breath as the small one slams the van's sliding side door shut behind them and locks it. "How'd I ever get them as a crew?" he laments as again the little guy struggles with the big garage door to close it.

Meanwhile, pushing the couple, the two big Uglys reach a large empty looking room. In the center are two chairs and table with no other apparent furniture. The room is cold and empty looking, even though boxes and crates line the walls. On two sides, large industrial windows with years of dirt and mud on them let in a hint of sun light. Charlotte Missing, the young lady, shivers from the austere and foreboding atmosphere. Even though she cannot see it, she can feel it and is even more frightened, if that is possible.

Rob Ebner, the young hooded male tries to break loose until the two larger ugly men put their hands on his shoulders and hold him square in his seat. Charlotte sobs and, gasping for air, hyperventilates. The boss man has had enough of her and yells at the small guy, "Go talk to her. Get her to stop sobbing, whining and shut up!"

Al, the power hungry leader, and his three ugly-ones stand around. As the captors replace the handcuffs on the young couple and lock them to the old rickety chairs, the young couple are completely confused. "What's going on? What do you want? Do you want money? I don't have much, but you can have whatever I have," the young man questions as he moves his hips toward the voices of his captors as if to gesture that it is all right for them to reach inside his pockets.

Both are kept hooded and told to keep silent. Charlotte continues to sob. One of the ugly ones steps toward her in an apparent attempt to console her. The little runt of a leader grabs his arm and makes a motion of not-to-help.

One of the big ugly mob guys seems to be allergic to the half inch of dust that covers everything and starts coughing. He grabs a bottle of water and quickly wets a cloth he pulls from his back pocket wrapping it around his mouth to help filter the dust. The little runt boss man just shakes his head in disgust saying, "One born every minute."

The little runt instructs one of them to take the cell phone from the Rob and call someone. Again, the 6'1" frame and muscles of this young man from under the hood yells out, "What's going on? Come on answer me." The little runt motions for one of the other ugly ones to say, "Tell us your mother's phone number." Rob jerks back in total darkness and loudly yells, "No, who the heck are you?"

But by this time, the guy with the phone has already opened the phone to the memory section of the phone book. He scans through the phone numbers in the memory and finds the one named "Mom." Smiling as he hits the dial button, he says to Al "It's Ok, I have it here - the i.c.e."

The cell phone starts to dial Mom's number. Everyone perks up to listen to the rings: one, two, three. Suddenly someone answers.

A beautiful lady sits at a desk. A nameplate in front her reads,

"Roberta (Bob) Ebner."

In a nice plush looking office, pulling her cell phone out of a small red purse, she sees Rob's phone number on her display. She answers her cell phone, "Hi Rob, anything new at your end?"

The kidnapper tries to muffle his voice but this woman has no idea who it is anyway. He tells her to go to her son's car at the park in the center of town, and look for a note on the front seat. In a threatening voice he directs her to, "Follow the instructions or else." As he hangs up the gang of Uglys snicker like little 3rd graders.

3.

Bob

Bob is uncertain what to think. She sits silently in her swivel chair for a moment seemingly in a daze and tells the lady next to her, Fran, that she has to go get a note from Rob's car for some unknown reason.

She exits the office, walks to a Bronco, thinking about the phone call she had just had, and casually gets in. Still in a daze she sits in the car without starting the engine. Two Teddy bears ride shotgun: Barney and Betty with button-eye wondering what Bob is doing then looking at each other quizzically. Bob starts the Bronco and drives out of the parking lot and heads toward the center of town where the park is located. She sees Rob's car and the park bench where it all started. She stops, hesitates and looks around as Barney and Betty watch her walk over to Rob's 1981 Mustang with college stickers on the back widow. She opens the driver's side door and notices a folded envelope. She picks it up and pulls out the note, which seems to be a cuddly pasted together message.

Using letters from the newspaper on yellow lined legal paper, the note reads, "Turn over everything about the 'SPECIAL WATER' within 24 hours or

'the kids will die'."

In total confusion, Bob grabs her cell phone and tries dialing the police department twice until she calms down and dials 911.

She quickly asks for Police Chief Rugger, an old family friend. He answers "Hello, Chief Rugger here. Can I help you?"

Bob, frantically says, "Buck, this is Bob Ebner, Rob and Charlotte have been kidnapped." She goes on to tell him about the note, the call and the car in the park.

Chief Rugger's face becomes stoic as he takes a slow deep breath of air. Something sounds strange in the Chief's voice. He explains that he can't do anything for at least twenty-four hours. At this point you can tell he really doesn't seem to care about her or Rob or Charlotte. He then tells her he will file a missing person's report and wants her to call him if anything new develops. Thanking her for the call, he hangs up on her.

After he hangs up, you can tell the Police Chief thinks it's just a trick of some kind and tells all of his officers that were listening, "Never mind. Go about your regular business." The Chief is an old friend and ex-lover of Bob's older sister, Angel Summit, and still holds a grudge about something, but why no feeling for the kids?

Bob, motionless, just stands next to her Bronco in a daze as the button eyes of Barney and Betty seem to have the same daze in them.

4.

18 Hours Later

By morning, Bob clearly spent the entire night calling all of Rob's friends and anyone else she can think of in an effort to piece all of this together.

Back at the old dusty factory/warehouse Rob's cell phone rings. One of the ugly's answers. Bob begs for more time and to have a "meeting" with them. In the background the men are laughing. The one on the phone explains to her that they have the kids and they're not going to have any kind of "funny meeting." Her time is running out and for her to turn over the secrets to the "Special Water" or the kids will be injected with a killer virus.

It becomes obvious to Big Al that Bob is trying to string the conversation along. He orders the ugly-one to get off the phone. He quickly obeys orders given to him by the little power hungry runt of a boss and hangs up.

5.

Deadline

The deadline has passed. The Uglys clamor around Big Al and all question him at the same time as to what they should do. Meanwhile, it seems Bob cannot do anything fast enough for these kidnappers. They no longer answer the cell phone, but laugh every time it rings. "Does Junior want to speak to his Mommy?" one of the Uglys taunts Rob.

The kidnappers threaten to inject Rob and his girlfriend Charlotte with some kind of virus if Bob does not do what they want. As they eye their watches, one slowly fills the syringes with some dark solution and prepares to inject the kids.

Rob tries to talk to them but is gagged and still has a hood over his head. Charlotte continues muffled screaming and yelling between her sobbing and hyperventilating but no one is listening. Her sobbing and moaning attracts the attention of one of them but Al keeps walking between Charlotte and the man with the sympathetic eyes. "Good

God, woman, shut up!." Big Al yells at her shaking his head. He wonders what her screams would be like without the hood over her and is thankful he is not Rob even though she is a major Babe.

The kids' arms have been taped to the chair arm, so no matter how strong and powerful Rob is he is helpless.

One of them calmly injects Rob's left arm and Rob yells, "Stop!" We see the pain on his face as the fluid is being pushed slowly into his vein and his protestations weaken. Surprisingly and compassionately, the ugly one places, a band-aid over the injected area and the little runt boss Al, makes a motion of, "How dumb that is?"

The ugly one sets up to repeat the action with Charlotte's arm as Rob's weakened yelling continues, to no avail. Charlotte's arm is injected and we can hear her sobbing cries of terror and a whiney noise as she slumps down in her chair. The little runt, Al, stops anyone from coming to her rescue.

6.

When It All Started

Bob, back in the Bronco, feels that her son hates her for things that they have argued about in the past few weeks. Still she sets out to save them with only the aid of Barney and Betty.

We see her making a map of something and addressing it to her husband, knowing this maybe "it." The park is in the middle of town and there is a mailbox at the edge of the park entrance where Bob drops the envelope in on her way to Rob's car.

Sitting in the Bronco next to Rob's car, Bob waits for two people, one a nurse friend, to help her drive Rob's car back to Beacon Crest Circle. She ponders the feelings of the characters Clint Eastwood (Dirty Harry) or Bruce Willis (Die Hard) play in their movies. But, "WATER STORM," her "Desert Storm," is all that matters.

She knows this nurse also has some connections that may help her find Rob and Charlotte.

During this wait the three of them, Bob, Barney and Betty, reflect back over the past four months when this terrible nightmare began.

It was the annual Easter Egg Hunt in the back yard just after a beautiful Easter morning service.

She remembers vividly that beautiful sunny morning in the small town of Vallivue Falls, an "All–America" town and that particular Easter morning.

In front of a stunning church nestled among this bedroom community we see the congregation standing out side in the sunlight, on the sidewalks and lawn laughing and talking with each other. All the ladies are dressed in beautiful colors of the rainbow and the gentlemen with ties to match.

The family of R. C. Ebner with their daughter Roberta (Berta), a first year student in college (not happy and ignoring as many others as possible) and his wife, Roberta (Bob), patiently waiting for their son Rob, a college senior, who is always late due to Charlotte his girlfriend, a well-built blonde who is incapable of thinking beyond a two minute span and unable to see beyond her nose.

Just then Alice, one of the finely dressed ladies, comes through the crowd calling out, "Hi Bob!" R. C. turns his head as his wife looks around him and answers, "Hi Alice!"

The ladies gossip about the reason for Rob's tardiness, at Charlotte's expense. Soon other female friends gather and everyone begins to laugh uproariously.

The sun is shining on all the beautiful colors of clothing and hats and the kids are running around the parents playing tag.

In the background Berta, ties to sneak out but she is quickly caught by R.C. Nicely dressed it is clear Berta is very uncomfortable and would rather be in dirty worn-out jeans, a low cut T-shirt, bra less, with too many rings, and five or six necklace's.

The front of the church and walkway leading to the front doors are almost overly decorated with flowers donated by the congregants. The colors are spectacular and the fragrance intoxicating. Both doors are propped open for parishioners to start to enter for the "after sunrise service."

Church bells chime from within as everyone starts filing through the beautiful flowers, through the double doors, to their seats - everyone, except of course for Rob and Charlotte, who have yet to arrive.

7.

Needed Hardware

It is the morning after the kidnapping. Bob drives to her parents' house to retrieve some of her guns she used as the President of the all male high school gun club.

The sixteen mile drive into another county north of Vallivue Falls is beautiful with trees lining most of the roadway and a few small vineyards in full bloom.

The driveway is about a mile long up the side of a hill to a beautiful majestic style house designed by Mom and Dad. Bob has the password for the gate to open. As she drives up the roadway you can see the worry in her face considering what she has to do.

Her parents aren't home so see uses the key they gave her and unlocks the door to the kitchen. Barney and Betty view the majestic valley of fields and vineyards while Bob enters the house, walks through the kitchen and down a long hall until she finally reaches her Dad's study.

Animal head trophies and the gun used in each hunt decorate the top of three walls. The fourth wall is all glass with a panoramic view of the valley below. To her right is dad's large roll up desk, closed and locked. Steel gun cabinets border each side: one for rifles; the other for both rifles and pistols.

Bob has the key to the one on the left. Dad always kept her guns in this one. She unlocks it, turns the handle and opens the double doors wide. Not all of them are hers but she is only interested in hers. She knows exactly what they will and can do. She has no desire of making any mistake. It is her son and his girlfriend. Any mistake could hurt one or both of them or an innocent.

Not knowing the full situation, she removes two rifles and a pistol, ammo for all three, some cleaning equipment, a few specially oiled towels, and a few of her gun mounts that hold rifles in place for target shooting.

She pulls her dad's chair over to the cabinet peering in trying to think of everything she would need and most of all what might happen.

The walls are decorated with her dad's military awards and a picture of dad and mom at a hospital where they first met. Alongside the hospital photograph is a picture of the first "The Big 5" sporting goods store her dad opened, his partners and he broadly smiling in the foreground.

Photographs on the rest of the walls depict high school and NRA trophies and pictures with Bob and her trophies and awards.

A smaller section on one wall has pictures and a crown encased in glass. This area is for Bob's old sister, Angel Summit, as prom queen and college beauty queen. There are more pictures of her sister in the hall and foyer. Although equally proud of Angel, Dad would say, "Not in the gun room."

Bob pauses again for a moment, not studying the pictures or trophies but in deep thought about what she needs to do. Guns are not toys and she remembers her dad teaching her what a bullet would do. First he took his smallest rifle, a 22 caliber, and held it up to a small limb of a tree and fired. Then showed the broken mangled limb to Bob and stated, "This is what a little 22 can do to bone the same size as your finger". Next he took his 303 British Enfield military rifle and did the same to a 3" limb saying, "There are no bones in the human body as big as this limb." The mangled pieces of the 3" limb were all shredded. The lesson was definitely learned.

She carefully locked everything up, put the chair back in place and wrote her Dad a note telling him which guns she had taken.

Bob exits the house, making sure the door was locked, and walks to her Bronco with all the guns and equipment in hand. Barney and Betty sit tall knowing they are riding shotgun to some of Bob's real guns and her expert marksmanship abilities.

Down the driveway, out the gate, watching to see it closes and locks behind the Bronco Bob returns to the park and Rob's car.

8.

Back To The Park

Bob wipes her eyes as her nurse friend pulls up to help with Rob's car. They grew up together and one of Bob's classmates was the nurse's older brother.

Before Bob can say anything or even get out of the Bronco the nurse tells Bob she will take care of the car and not to worry and strongly, as a friend, says, "Bob, promise me you will go to 'Momma's Place.' You know that restaurant on the other side of town."

Bob looks shocked and questions, "Why?" The nurse responds, "Bob I know you. You're going after the kids. Don't answer. Just go there and Big Momma will help you."

Bob, stunned for a moment, knows her friend well enough to listen. She nods her head, wipes her eyes, checks with Barney and Betty and drives off to the other side of town.

"Momma's Place" is off the beaten path and is only known to locals as a restaurant for great ribs and chicken. Bob and her husband have not had the pleasure of eating there, but know its reputation well.

Bob parks the Bronco off to the side of the road and pauses, still with some small salty tears running down her cheeks. This is known as the tough side of town but Barney and Betty sit tall and plan on guarding the Bronco until Bob returns.

Sitting in front of "MOMMA"S PLACE," she recalls that morning in church. In the front pew we see Bob's Mom and Dad, the retired Army General, sitting at attention and her husband's Mom and Dad, a conservative accountant. Her in-laws are a very nice relaxed couple. R. C. followed in his father's footsteps. In the next pew with Bob and R. C. is their daughter, Berta and Bob's sister Angel Summit, perfectly dressed after spending just two hours with her hair and make-up, Rob and Charlotte run in and sit in the seats Dad and Mom have saved for them in the front pew just as the Easter service begins.

9.

Rob's and
Charlotte's Apartment

Charlotte, feeling guilty and acting sheepishly for them being late, reflects on the reason. At their apartment, Charlotte runs around trying to get ready for church and at the same time hastily tries to rush an over the counter pregnancy test kit before leaving for church. Rob has no idea Charlotte is taking the test as she hides in the bathroom, making sounds like she is washing, flushing or doing something active and not just waiting for the test to finish.

Rob, dressed and pacing in front of the door, dangles his car keys and waits for what he thinks is a necessary finishing touch to Charlotte's makeup.

In the bathroom Charlotte paces back and forth from her hair and the mirror to the small plastic pregnancy test kit. Finally giving up on the test and believing she is not pregnant, she wraps the kit in facial tissue and throws it in the trash. Rob, anxious to get to the church, doesn't have time for questions as Charlotte runs toward him. They both run to the car as we see the test kit unfold indicating, "Yes, you are pregnant."

Rob and Charlotte arrive and find their seats just in time to witness the baptism of a friend's daughter.

As the service reaches near the end, the congregation waits for the announcement of the annual Easter egg party for all to attend at R.C. and Bob's house.

10.

The Egg Hunt

Ah, the Easter party brings out the best in everyone. It has no color or religious barriers, just fun for all. The only unwritten rule is to help anyway you can with the children, the food, or the elderly in the lounge chairs and to HAVE FUN.

Many of Bob's inventions are used and seen for the first time. Some people come to the party just to see what she has created since last year. From the past, a hamburger flipper that grills the burgers on the hot gas grill and automatically flips them and when cooked puts them on a platter. Another one   takes ground hamburger and cooks it in a chamber separating and draining the grease for sloppy-Joes, spaghetti sauce and Coney-dogs.

Hunting for hidden eggs always seems to bring out the best in everyone, even daughter Berta, who by now has changed into her what see calls her "C.V.'s," complete with the ear rings, rings on all fingers, a dozen necklaces along with clothes that most would have tossed out months ago. For this event, everyone is shown respect, no matter how different. Even though Berta wants to rebel, this day is different, this is Easter and egg hunting.

Celebrity impersonators play with the children, engaging in "magic" tricks, balloon twisting, face and tile painting. "Charlie Chaplin" swaggers around with his cane twirling in the air. "Roy Rogers and Dale Evens" with their dog "Bullet" amaze children with roping tricks. Pony rides are given by the masked "Lone Ranger" and his Indian sidekick "Tonto," and many more.

In front of the house what could be a traffic jam is averted by volunteers and police directing traffic. People dropping off food, children and those individuals who find walking difficult are allowed through the throngs. Everyone else is directed to the parking at the near by junior high school with shuttle service from a local airport bus shuttle company bringing people to the party. The owner of the shuttle service is already at the party and helping out at the grill. The shuttle bus owner also knows a portable potty company that donates several "stalls" set up at the neighbor's driveway.

The Beacon Crest property is pie shaped. With the neighbors' lots, the yards are open and end at a small forest of trees, flowers and a little stream. In their backyard, Bob built a small pond with room for her water inventions, including a water wheel to a water pump powered by itself, a solar fan keeping the breeze going and a windmill.

Today the yard serves another purpose. Colored eggs hidden by many of the guests under, Berta's direction, give the backyard a more whimsical feeling. Berta says it takes her back to her younger days and loves to do the hiding of the eggs with the others. Her friends think it is lame and prefer to be alone in the trees and bushes to watch.

Today the yard serves another purpose. Colored eggs hidden by many of the guests under Berta's direction, give the backyard a more whimsical feeling. Berta says it takes her back to her younger days and loves to do the hiding of the eggs with the others. Her friends think it is lame and prefer to be alone in the trees and bushes to watch.

Everyone seems to bring something to add to the assortment of ethnic foods from all around the world and desserts line a 30' table covered with tents to keep out pesky bugs.

Steaks, burgers, hot dogs, cooked ground hamburger for sloppy Joes, Coney-dogs or spaghetti, tacos, gyros, chicken for sandwiches, chicken stew, pork chops, pulled pork, ribs, sliced deli meat, two kinds of meat loaf, anything and everything seemed to be available. There were even dishes for vegetarians. Fathers, son, uncles and neighbors and the shuttle bus owner staffed the grills. The ladies watched the salads, deserts, potatoes, noodles and drinks.

Potatoes were available cooked in all different ways: baked, fried, mashed, wedged with three different flavors, 4 separate noodles dishes and 3 rice dishes and that did not even include the twelve different styles of salads. There was, a veritable banquet all in the backyard of the Beacon Crest property.

In front of the house the ice cream truck that normally travels through the neighborhood every evening sat still, waiting until Moms were certain the kids had some nutrition first before passing out the creamy, sweet and chocolate dipped goodies. Chuck, the ice cream man, was a paraplegic has a special set up in the truck for his chair. He loves the rewards he receives from the smiles on the kids' faces when he drives through the mall or grocery store or at his daytime job as the crossing guard at the local grade school when they chat with him.

Bob and R.C. take a moment to sit on a blanket under a tree and just observe all the day and the city has to offer. The children are all happy and playing, the adults are talking and laughing. The weather for the day is slightly warm with a cool breeze and clear blue skies. Lawns are freshly mowed and the air smells of the gentle fragrance of spring flowers.

Even in economically tumultuous times, Vallivue Falls seems to be unaffected. Just a couple blocks away a main highway goes north and south through the west edge of town and another goes east and west across the north side. They bring travelers, trucking, buses and good outside sources of business and income. With in a few minutes we have skiing in the mountains and lakes for boating and fishing and the ocean is just a few hours away. The town could not be more idyllic.

II.

Momma's Place

In the Bronco at the restaurant, Bob wipes small tears from her cheek remembering the annual Easter party. Those are the memories that make one a wealthy person, "Black, white, yellow, brown, red, green, purple and little Gray's from Mars are all welcome."

Bob grew up in this town. Why, then, is she so afraid of going in? Mustering all of the courage of the Lion from the "Wizard of Oz" she opens the door of the Bronco. Bob pauses remembering "Big Momma" is both well respected and feared The "lion" inside her says, "I trust my friend." Bob walks with trepidation to the front door.

This area is better known as the dark side of town, but the big red sign reads;

"MOMMA'S PLACE"
World famous Ribs and Chicken
Welcome – All"

Bob looks around noting that even for the "dark side of town," the restaurant is in a nice location next to a shopping complex with a big parking lot. Still, Bob's hairs on her neck stand up as she pauses for another moment remembering her Dad, Col. Max's words of wisdom, "Trust your real friends for they will cover your flanks." In the military world that is important.

Bob opens the door, walks in and is greeted and treated as if everyone knew she was coming. She is than escorted to a table at a back corner, next to an old-fashioned looking jukebox playing the c.d., "Unforgettable." "Would you care for some ice tea, coca-cola or something stronger while you wait?" her greeter asked politely as if she were in a fine restaurant. She nervously says, "No thank you," even though her throat was a big giant cotton ball.

Moments later "Big Momma" comes out of the kitchen and sits with Bob. Bob looks up, completely surprised. Bob knows her as "Aunt Helen." a lady who always brings 5 or 6 kids to the Easter party along with dozens of the most decorative eggs, gifts, party hats for kids, food and many other things for celebration.

"Aunt Helen!" Bob exclaims. "Hi Bob," Helen says in return, "Nice to see you in my neighborhood." Big Momma is known as a woman of few but poignant words. "Heard you need some help. A friend told me. Yes, I know where the scum buckets are. Any plans?"

Bob, still speechless for a moment says, "I've got to get them back safely, Rob and Charlotte I mean. If you can tell where they're at, I can go there and shoot my way in if I have to. The police won't help. It's my son and his girlfriend. They don't need to be part of my problem."

Big Momma smiles and replies, "I've helped raise 18 kids in this neighborhood. Your parties have always made it easy to show them friendship between our worlds. Anything I can do to help you is yours. My right hand, "Tiny" will take you to the kidnappers and assist you any way you want."

"But I don't want anyone else involved," Bob protests.

Momma responds, "That's Tiny behind you." Bob turns to see this tree trunk of a man standing close behind her and he looks down and says, "Ma'am!" with a smile.

Bob quivers for a moment. After adjusting to the tingling of her skin and clearing of her throat she faintly acknowledges Tiny with a nod and smile.

Big Mommy continues, "OH, that's part of the deal, Honey. You have your Easter party for all friends - even the little Grays from Mars.

Friends help friends. Trust me, he will help, and he can call me if you need anything else. Now you go and do your thing." Big Momma says it all with conviction and as she leaves the table tells her servers to fix some "To Go" bags of food and drinks for Bob and Tiny. For what they are about to do, they need food and lots of it.

Bob sits silently with a look of confusion about what just happened then a look of a "Positive Mental Attitude" comes over her from the great teacher Dale Carnegie. Bob and Tiny leave with the bags of food and Tiny opens the Bronco door for Bob and then goes around to the passenger side, opens the door and finds Bob moving Barney and Betty onto the back seat. He sits quietly with a smile and scans all the covered guns and equipment in the back seat along with Barney and Betty's button eyes staring at him.

12.

The Bronco

It was just three days before last Easter that Bob sat outside the garage in the1985 Bronco Il she had just bought.

The standard color of dark brown and tan vehicle was owned by a 75-year young lady who loved the idea of four-wheel drive. Although it was never used, the Bronco was equipped with electric windows and locks and a trailer hitch, but no air-conditioning. She told Bob when she bought it that her son worked at a quick oil station and changed the oil every month. Bob didn't know why. Even though it was 20 some years old, the Bronco had only 62,000 miles on it. The body was super clean and only the driver's seat had ever been used.

Ever since she picked it up she has been talking to the family about going up into the mountains with her to do some old style gold prospecting and camping. The trip had almost become an obsession with Bob. The family, far less enthused, run and hide when the words "Bronco," "camping" and "prospecting" are used in the same sentence.

13.

The Family

On the patio in the back of the house we see the family table with honored parents, quests, elders from the community, grandparents and great-grandparents and, in a special area for babies in their strollers, attended by young ladies of baby sitting age with a few young mothers.

In the background we hear R.C.'s and Bob's music from the 12 wireless speakers planted around the back yard playing an old classic of "Love is a Many-Splendored Thing" followed by Easter classics.

Ken Smith, a local DJ, who also comes to participate and have fun, provides music, announces the winners of the egg contests and passes out the prizes even though we know all the children win something. There are hundreds of prizes donated by many of the guests. Ken's wife is the custodian of the prizes and puts them in age brackets from one to six.

At one of the tables sit R.C.'s Mom and Dad, John and Sara Ebner. John is a retired CPA and CFO of a large computer-manufacturing firm. Sara is a retired bank officer. As an account and banker they are quite conservative and now live in a Sun City retirement community in the Phoenix area and drive a small Hybrid. They always go on 2 one-week vacations each year, to the same place. At home they drive a golf cart to the store down the special lane for carts with a 15 mph speed limit.

Next to the Ebners are Bob's Mom and Dad, Army Col. Ray Maxwell, Ret., and Judy Maxwell. After 20 years in service, Max and four of his military buddies started a sporting goods store and named it "Big 5 Sporting Goods" for the five of them. The concept grew in the next thirty years. Twenty stores later they were still doing quite well. Max and his buddies guessed, and rightly so, that all of that survival training was good for something. Judy Maxwell, an Army nurse when they first met, was a nurse until retiring. They live in a very large house on 220 acres in the next county and travel in their motor home extensively.

At the next table sits the very beautiful, older sister, Angel Summit. As always, Angel is dressed to the max with lots of gold and is drinking Perrier. Angel is no miser when it comes to spreading her wealth for Bob's party. Whatever she needs: sisters are sisters. Even though Angel is into make-up and Bob into inventions they are true sisters. She was raised the same as Bob, but was a cheerleader in high school and beauty queen in college. Right out of college she married one of her college boyfriends who was hard working and had fallen into lots of money giving her permission to be the high maintenance queen she is today. Even though she put on airs, Bob knows that Angel truly loved her husband who passed away last year with cancer. Her shopping sprees are small compensation for the great loss in her life.

Son, Robert Charles Ebner, II, sits next to Grandpa Max, the one he really looks up too. At 6'1" and about 230,

Rob is graduating from college where he had a football scholarship. An injury is keeping him from a pro-football career. He is living off campus with his college girlfriend Charlotte Jean Missing, A tall blond who is going to graduate next year with a degree in something, or not.

A seat next to Angle is open for Roberta Cynthia Ebner, (Berta) not on the patio, she is out hiding eggs and playing with the kids.   When it's not Easter, she is a first year college student of some sort, rebelling against everything: teachers, books, studying, cloths, you name it. Wild parties and drugs seem to be a must for her crowd.   But on Easter it is all about the kids. Bob looks at Berta and how good she is with little children.

Wistfully she thinks, "Gee, maybe she will make a great mother someday after all."

Berta gets an extra kick out of the small gray coveralls designed like tuxedos Max Katz had made for his sons and nephews. They have been coming to the Easter party every year for almost ten years: never missed a one. Max is one of the attorneys at the law firm where R.C. works and, after going to the synagogue on Saturday, Easter egg hunting is not part of their tradition. Max always says that he is bringing his little Gray's from Mars, and that's when Berta understands more about life, family and true friendship.

14.

Bob's Think Tank

Rob takes Charlotte around and showing her the many gadgets his mom has invented and built in her work shop in the garage and says, "Welcome to Mom's Think Tank." Although compact, Charlotte is amazed at the small steel fabrication shop, carpenter shop and auto mechanics shop with about every tool you can imagine.

Although the garage is doublewide and double long, the side next to the house and door to the laundry area and kitchen is the only area where R.C. can park a car. Cabinets hang on walls from the door to the laundry room all the way around to the far garage door. Under each cabinet are pegboard panels for Bob's tools hanging neatly. Each is outlined so that borrowers know the proper replacement site for each tool.

Under the peg board panels, the workbench spans an entire wall of the garage. Even though all the area is the same table height we see sections that roll out for the welder, the table saw, a floor model drill press and band saw: all are built onto a table that rolls. With the exception of her desk all the other tool benches roll in and out.

Off to the center of the parking bays we see a '62 Lincoln Continental sitting on 8"x8" wooden blocks. The car is shifted off center into the center of the garage giving more room for the workshop.

For the past five years Bob has been rebuilding it for driving to church, on vacations and shopping. Even on blocks, everything works and it has been primed and ready for the final paint job. It's going to be all white along with the powder blue leather seats, dash, carpet and interior of the doors.

Above all this we see a large plank hanging down from the ceiling and the words carved out:

"BOB'S THINK TANK"

This sign hangs lower than the bikes and lawn tools that hang in neatly arranged areas for use when needed. The heavier tools are retrieved through a winch system designed and built by Bob to lower or raise them when needed. Bob is quite proud of the ingenious method she developed of raising and lowering the heavy tools she needs. All she has to do is sit at her desk and move her finger. After all, why run the risk of hurting her back?

Everyone always wants a demonstration of this so Rob has to show Charlotte how it works. When Rob sits in Bob's chair the music comes on automatically and they hear, "Muskrat Love." Rob shakes his head in disbelieve that the song is one of his parents' favorites. Charlotte's eyes light up as she exclaims, chiding and tickling Rob, "Ooooh, can you make one of these for us? Just think, I won't have to ask you to reach for a pot and pan every again."

"Don't!" Rob says, looking at her sternly, "Stop tickling me and no. I don't mind your asking help to reach a heavy pot or pan. Anyway, it is nice to know you need me for something besides the obvious," Rob retorts grabbing Charlotte around her waist from behind. She turns and they kiss.

15.

The Trip

Once again, Bob asks the family about going on a trip with the SUV to pan for gold. This has been a long time dream of hers and, given what she does for the family, she thinks it is only a slight sacrifice on their part and knows deep in her heart that once there, they will have the time of their lives. One by one, Bob approaches each member.

Bob's dad, Col. Max, thinks it is a great idea but he has, "been-there-done-that," and is not interested in taking an adventure trip at his age. Her mom thinks, "that it is dumb even at Bob's age," and most certainly not her thing.

R. C., always busy with office work, laughs at the idea, and wants Bob to stay home due to a flu bug that has hit him and will undoubtedly strike his beautiful wife. Berta thinks anything an older person does is dumb. Rob thinks Mom is out of her mind and she should sell this relic of a SUV. Charlotte thinks it is a great idea and would like to go along but she isn't sure what a tent is and gold comes from the jewelry store already in circles, so why would anyone "pan" for it as if it were fish. She muses whether once panned if it is then fried.

Bob really wants to relax in the woods and not baby sit a 21- year old blonde, or any of the rest of them. She secretly thinks it would be good for them to spend some time on their own without her and certainly she could use the R&R, particularly after the Easter party. It is only out of a feeling of guilt that she even bothers to ask them.

Asking her sister, Angle, would be out of the question. Angle's idea of camping includes inviting her hair stylist, manicurist, valet, driver, chef, and housemaid: the essentials.

As for R. C.'s parents, who live in a guarded senior community with their high speed golf carts, a trip to the grocery store feels like an out of town excursion.

Friends believe that the most Bob will find on the trip is a good case of poison ivy, bugs and snakes, but no gold.

Undaunted, Bob starts to pack the Bronco for the trip. She laughs at herself with the realization that she is not a total pioneer. Here she is packing a tent, sleeping bag, matches, sterno in case she cannot start a fire, pans, dishes, silverware, cups, thermos, coke, milk, apple juice, and all the foods she would normally eat.

Bob next loads a few of her guns and ammo for target shooting including two 22 rifles: one with a standard 22 open site; the other one of her expensive ones for target shooting with a scope, both with good rifle cases, and a handgun and holster for practice and safety.

The Friday after Easter, Bob wraps up all the small details at her travel agency, frustrated that she was much busier than she thought she would be. It was as though her customers knew she's trying to sneak out early and they didn't want her to go.

As it is, the drive will take at least 5 to 6 hours, if she can beat the worst of the Friday night rush hour traffic, and wants to settle in before dark, at about 8 P.M.

She takes a last look around at her little business, located in a little shopping complex with a big sign:

"EBNER'S TRAVELS -

From The Mountains To The Sea"

From the outside, the storefront is a large glass pane and one door leading into this large room with a counter and two desks behind it. One large desk at the far end of the room appears to be the boss' desk. All are "L" shaped with the standard computer and travel brochures flanked by chairs at each desk for the comfort of the clients. Behind the back desk is a partition in front of the kitchen area with a small coffee maker, refrigerator, cupboard for cups etc., and a small lunch table with four chairs.

Just as she gets ready to leave R. C. stops by the office with a gift for her.

On the dash of the Bronco we see two dolls, one a bobble-headed doll that looked like one of Bob's dogs, Bugsy, a white German Shepard. He had passed away last year at age 13. Obviously this Bugsy was just as well loved with a faded, cracked and chipped body and the spring from the bobble head sprung. It had been her "right hand man" since she was in the high school gun club.

The other doll is a Teddy bear named Barney. Bugsy and Barney rode shotgun with Bob wherever she traveled, until now. It was time for Bugsy to retire. The gift from R.C. is Bugsy's replacement, a female Teddy bear, "Betty," They buckle Barney and Betty together in the passenger seat.

R. C. and Bob are still high school lovers at heart and in the parking lot it shows as passing cars beep there horns at the "love birds" kissing and hugging as the Bronco radio plays the Mama Cass tune, "Dream a Little Dream of Me."

16.

On The Way

Bob hops into the Bronco and drives away as they both wave to each other.

On her way out of town she stops in to get a last minute fill-up of gas at the near-by station where many old friends hang out and make small talk.

The station is one of the newer modern ones with 6 regular pumps and 2 with gas and diesel fuel. Inside is the small travelers' grocery store and make-your-own-lunch restaurant counter with tables to sit and relax.

Bob went to school with some of the ladies. Some of the younger mothers with kids had been at her Easter party last weekend. All know her plans to pan for gold and some applaud her for realizing her life's dream. Others, mostly men, heckle her for doing the things they don't have the guts to do.

Two of her friends getting gas are nurses on their way to their work. They think it is great that she has the nerve to go off on her own. They tell the guys, "If you had any hair on your chest you would be going." The ladies laugh. The heckling is quieted.

Along with gas, Bob fills up with more snacks and carbonated drinks for the trip. The Bronco is packed so tightly that most of the goodies have to go on the front floor passenger side or in Barney and Betty's lap.

17.

The Drive

The long drive begins through newly planted farms and fields with a beautiful landscape of mountains and majestic pines lining the slopes in the distance. The sky is as blue as a picture post card with just a few clouds peeking through in the treetops.

Bob, dressed in some of her work cloths from the think tank, drinks a can of Coke she takes from the beverage holder built into the small consul between the seats. In the front passenger seat sit Barney and Betty buckled in for safety and clutching the snacks from the gas station. Bob talks to them and answers for them as their button eyes seem to watch over her and heads nod in agreement when questioned.

The trip is uneventful except for the last hours of driving down this mountainside dirt road. Even in the best conditions, the road requires full attention. Tonight it has been half washed out from recent rains and the edge of the road is nothing but a cliff. Bob is an excellent driver and the good old four-wheeler keeps on going. She remembers, briefly, the Bondurant driving school Col. Max insisted she take and is now thankful she had.

At the bottom of this mountain is a stream shown on the map and as a surprise, a concrete bridge across the stream. Bob stops to look around and sees the bridge, mostly covered with moss, was built in 1955. It still looks sound. Bob is relieved she will not have to forge the stream.

On the other side of the bridge, she looks around and thinks to herself, "This is a good spot." She wanders around and finds an old path, heavy with brush and small trees but can see it was once a trail. It goes back into the woods farther than she is able to see. Bob returns to the Bronco and drives into the woods.

18.

Campsite

This is it, "Go For It," is her motto. She locks in her front hubs for total four-wheel drive, puts the transmission in four-wheel low and drives, slowly, through the brush and trees that are so thick that she can only see about 20' ahead. Limbs slap the side of the Bronco wiping off some of the road dirt. After about a mile she comes to a clearing over looking the stream.

"Wow, this is perfect," she whispers to herself. Barney and Betty look out the window and nod that they like what they see. Bob exits the Bronco and just stands looking at the view. "What a Valley! What do you think Barney and Betty?" The clearing is about the size of an average front and back yard. Weeds and grass are 6" high and easy to flatten down with her feet. The tree line around the site has openings in each direction with magnificent views of the valley and mountains. "Really beautiful!" Bob exclaims.

Bob had made good time on the road. It is still about an hour before sundown. She unpacks the tent and equipment. After about 30 minutes of setting up on the east edge of the opening, just inside the tree line, she finds a small trickle of water that drips onto a flat rock near her campsite. She places her cup under the water and waits for the cup to fill. The water looks clear and is cold as if it had just run from the top of the mountain. Still, Bob tests the water before taking a sip – always safety first. This small trickle goes down to the stream about 200 feet away. She tries a little sample. It tastes great. "Hmmmm, nice and cold," she shares with Barney and Betty. They agree.

As she views the area and the stream looking 200 yards in either direction she sneezes and coughs from the runny nose and the flu bug that has been working it's way through the house for the last few days. "Great! Now I get sick," she laments. From experience Bob knows to set up a make shift "Outhouse" for her little "home." All her Girl Scout training comes back.

Off to one side she finds a log and clears the front and back of it off for this comfort and gathers small bushes placing them on the sides for privacy down to the stream. She pulls out a roll of her favorite tissue and blows her nose and wipes some of the flu bug away.

Once the campsite is all set up, Bob engages in a little R&R with a past love, target shooting. She sets up her two rifles on a tree stump over looking a beautiful stream and selects some leaves of a tree on a bank about 175 yards up stream as her targets.

19.

Mountain Man

This is the real R&R that she has missed for years. Bob loads the rifles, drinks some of the water that has been dripping into her cup, wipes her nose from the flu bug that is still eating at her and looks through the scope of her 22 rifle, aiming at the leaves.

What she doesn't know is just a few feet away from her target of leaves is a big bearded mountain man taking a bath, in his birthday suit.

After the first shot he stays low in the water thinking someone was aiming at him. Startled he exclaims, "What the?" But, after more leaves are blasted away he knows it is just target practice by one or more shooters. It is apparent he doesn't want anyone to know he is in the woods, as if he is hiding from something or someone.

A full box of shells later obliterating the poor leaves, she relaxes, feeling joyful and says to herself, "It must be time for something to eat and than just a good night's sleep."

Bob gets up and carries her rifles back to camp when her stomach begins to roar. Barney and Betty, who have been moved to the tent and are watching over her sleeping bag, nod in agreement.

The mountain man waits in his bath water for whomever was shooting to stop and leave the area before he ventures out of the stream. He peers around from behind some of the rocks to see if they were gone. Uncertain how many intruders there are to his peaceful existence, with stealth, he gets out of the water, dresses and starts his trek across the steam to observe Bob's campsite.

Dressed in full camouflaged hunting clothes to blend in with the forest and armed with his .357 Magnum handgun loaded and ready for any intruders at his side, the mountain man sits and patiently watches Bob. He looks for anyone that could or would give away his hideout.

Back at camp, Bob sips more water. With this flu bug getting to her, she hurriedly makes her way to the make shift 'outhouse' she had set-up earlier and proceeds to "lose all of her cookies." Sipping more water to wash away the bad taste left in her mouth, she keeps working on some small camping gear. Bob notices that her mind is not clear as she reworks the gear she had attempted to assemble and remarks to herself, "Boy that water tastes good. Very refreshing!" Barney and Betty nod.

By this time the big mountain man is at the campsite, just next to the outhouse. Thinking the coast was clear and checking everything out, he is surprised when Bob comes back. Bob runs into the outhouse, passed Mountain Man but doesn't see him. She is desperately trying to make it into the outhouse before she loses it again.

With his .357 drawn and ready, and surprised that Bob had not seen him, Mountain Man holds back to see what was going on. This time when Bob uses the 'outhouse' she wishes she had dug two holes. She pulls her pants down and lets loose with some of the nastiest smelling stuff she had ever known possible, right in front of the big guy. With a definite look of disgust on his face, Mountain Man is more eager to retreat from the smell than hide himself from Bob. From the smell of her, it is clear that her distress was more important than shooting him.

As Bob staggers back to camp feeling relieved and two pounds lighter, Mountain Man, determines that she is camping out by herself. He is still reeling from the embarrassment of seeing Bob half naked running to the outhouse and the horrendous odor emanating from it. Has he really been away from civilization so long that he had forgotten how odious it was?

In less than fifteen minutes, while Bob is trying to sleep, she wanders two more times to the outhouse, each time having a sip of water to wash out the bad taste in her mouth.

After the fourth trip her whole body just relaxes and she falls asleep in seconds, completely and totally, just like a baby, out like a light and body like an old dead log.

20.

Bath

By morning Bob feels great, no flu bug and no runs. She has a glancing thought about the water as she goes on about making the campsite a home for her and her closest friends, Barney and Betty, for the next few enjoyable days of relaxation.

She hikes through the hills and valleys up and down the mountains on both sides of the stream. Constantly hearing noises of footsteps, but believing the sound to be from a deer or other large animal, she doesn't worry. Just on the safe side, she pats her trusty sidearm holstered at her hip and shifts the weight of her rifle on her back.

After several hours of hiking, and an occasional target shooting, she fills her canteen with fresh water, takes a long swig of the cold clear water and feels great. She still wonders about the footsteps she hears, uncertain if it is wind or animal.

By late afternoon Bob feels itchy and dirty from hiking and crawling around the spring. It is time to enjoy a bath. She remembers a perfect spot for a bath she had seen on one of her trips down to see the remains of the leaves from her first days' targets practice. Bob gathers up her soaps including the Fels-Naptha for any poison ivy, shampoo and brushes, etc. and wanders down to that perfect spot in the river with the natural built-in "tub." She looks around to see if someone is watching but knows there can't be anyone.

Feeling secure that she is alone, Bob begins to drink in all of the beauty of the sun, foliage and water in the stream. The water is cold at first but soon Bob's body temperature adjusts and she begins to relax, just lays back and floats while all her troubles flow down stream. With a deep sigh she thinks, "What a way to live!" Leisurely shampooing her hair, rinsing it three times Bob then washes it with the Fels just in case she runs into poison ivy.

Little does she know that the big mountain man was just about to take his bath when she intruded. He stays silent, watches and waits for his turn. Meanwhile, Bob is unaware of his watchful eye and engages in "sun worship follies" as she plays in the stream. It is all he can do to keep from laughing.

Her skin finally starts to wrinkle and "prune" from all the soaking. She takes that as a hint that it is time to dry off, dress and head back to camp. It takes her almost twenty minutes before finishing her beauty regimen. She laughs at herself thinking, "Now why I am bothering with all of this stuff. As if anyone is going to see me." How much longer it would have taken Charlotte, let alone Angel!

The mountain-man had dozed off while waiting. Hearing her getting ready to leave, he wakes up but stays motionless and quiet so he can have his daily bath without any interruption.

Back at the camp, when Bob is not hiking, she reads and sketches new ideas and inventions for her "think tank" room. She uses the same techniques she had used since high school in lab notebooks, jotting down notes, always dating each page and including news item notations to help mark the dates. This special book was marked, "Ideas Book #17." Over the years she has filled up 16 other books.

Six magnificent days had passed and it is time to head home. As she starts packing up for the trip home she fills every container she has in the Bronco that will hold water. "If nothing else matters it's still great tasting water," she says to Barney and Betty. They nod.

21.

Trip Home

On her way home she marks the map so she can return to this "Garden of Eden" some day in the near future.

She drives back to the 1955 bridge and recalls the washed out dirt road she came in on was bad. Thinking it might be faster to go through the bridge and up the other way, she pauses and drives across the bridge and starts up. It starts to look worse. The washed out areas are as big as the Bronco. If the pot holes stay this big it won't be too bad, but some are about half the size of the Bronco. Up and down and left and right goes the Bronco. She stops and gets out, locks in the hubs and takes a good look.

One of the problems she sees is turning around if it gets any worse. She gets back in and starts up the hill slowly. After about 100 yards she stops again and takes another look. She can see areas that have no road at all.

Being alone she does not want any major problem so she makes the decision to back up far enough to turn around and go back down to the bridge and out the way she came in. This is not going to be easy. The road that is drivable is only one car width. She slowly backs up with her head sticking out the window. As incredulous as it seems, Bob is certain she hears footsteps. She looks at Barney and Betty and says, "Whoever it is probably won't even help me if we get stuck!"

Finally she sees a slightly wider spot and attempts to turn the Bronco around. In the middle of a 9' pot hole she turns and turns and turns, forward and backward, until she has it going down hill. Some of the times she is only inches from going off the side of the road and cliff. As she drives back to the stream and bridge, her mind is wondering about the strange noises, footsteps, the fact that the hair on the back of her neck stood up and she the eerie feeling that she had been watched.

The Bronco hits a deep sharp hole that brings her back to reality with a quick jerk of her head and nose almost hitting the stirring wheel. Bob instantly begins to shake with the reality that she really needs to pay attention to what she is doing, as if her life depended on it because her life depended on it.

Slowly and much more carefully, Bob crosses the bridge. She suddenly stops and remembers she wanted to take a picture of the 1955 bridge and this beautiful valley. As she snaps the digital camera she says, "Thank you bridge, see you again someday," unlocks her hubs and drives up the washed out road knowing the cliff side is now on her passenger side of the Bronco and harder to see the edge. After an hour or so she's back on real pavement and on her way back to civilization, refreshed and relaxed.

22.

Return

Upon her return Bob finds R.C. in bed, ill with the flu. Co-employees who did not want to work close to him at the office had sent him home from work early.

Bob heats water from her hiking trip on the stove to make him some tea. She carries the steeping tea and a cup and saucer on a tray into the bedroom, sets it down on the night stand next to the bed, fluffs his pillow, turns on the radio that's been playing "Moon River" and tries to help him get comfortable. He looks up and with his eyes nearly closed and says, "Thanks, Honey, " as the radio starts playing "This Guy's in Love With You."

Bob nods and quietly leaves the room. On her way to the garage to unload the camping equipment she thinks to herself that R.C. was ill before she left on her trip and he still was, poor fellow.

R.C. drinks some of the tea and moment's later runs to the bathroom with the same reaction Bob had in the woods.

He then goes back to the bedroom where he tries to rest and sips more tea. In just a few minutes he returns to the bathroom and repeats the process, several times. The smell is the worst odor he has ever had the displeasure to experience. So pervasive, the smell is sufficient to make him run back to the bathroom and heave. Suddenly, and in disbelief, he feels normal and even feels like jogging. The radio disc jockey seems to know just what to play as R. C. hears Louis Armstrong's "What a wonderful world."

Bob is in the garage for an hour thinking R.C. is sleeping when suddenly he comes out with just his rob and slippers on and is feeling great. After a kiss he thanks her for the tea and says whatever she put in it did the trick. It made him feel great and he got rid of the nastiest stuff in his stomach and rear-end that anyone could ever produce. Bob stands in wonder as she puts camping gear away.

R.C. opens the back door to the 1962 Lincoln Continental that Bob has been rebuilding for the passed five years. Both have been joking about this "big boat" and R.C. calls out, "Bob, do you remember what we've always joked about doing in the back seat of this boat?" She laughs, blushes and exclaims, "Dirty old man," with a twinkle in her eye.

He walks over to her, gently holds her hand and says, "Well how about now? You've been away for seven days and I feel great. The kids aren't here and we don't have to go to work tomorrow."

R.C turns on the radio to some of their favorite old time rock and roll love songs as it plays, "You belong to me," and gently leads her by the hand to the back door of the Lincoln that opens backwards, called suicide doors. He bends her over backwards and plants a soft-sensual-sexual loving kiss on her that she can't refuse as the radio changes to, "Hold Me, Thrill Me, Kiss Me," by Mel Carter.

Dropping the robe he has on, he shuffles his feet to toss the slippers. Both Bob and R.C. look like teenagers trying to hide from parents as they crawl into the back seat of the car. "Our own private "lovers' lane," R.C. remarks as they steam up the windows for the next few hours. Bob giggles and Barney and Betty, who are sitting in the Bronco in full view of the Lincoln, nod to the tune "Moon River" on the radio.

23.

The Next Morning

After a long night of "rolling-in-the-hay," Bob and R.C. wake up in their bed, completely happy and full of energy to music from their clock radio of "Oh What a Night." Laughing and playing with each other Bob whispers into R. C.'s ear, "You really are a dirty old man." R. C. responds, "Why don't you go camping every week? I like your mood when you come home, you sex kitten." He grabs her as they kiss again and again, like they did under the bleachers in high school.

The noise of her parents' radio playing Sonny and Cher's, "I Got You, Babe" and them making love woke Berta. She stumbles out of her bedroom and looks at her parents, the two teenagers, doing everything except making love on the kitchen counter. They don't even notice Berta has walked into the bedroom until she begins to make gagging noises and, grumbling under her breath, says, "Oh, please! You two are too old for that, or at least get a room." R.C. and

Bob look at each other and laugh. Doesn't she realize they are in their room?

Berta stumbles back to her room and slams the door. Bob and R. C. can't stop laughing from seeing her face with her big eyes partly bloodshot and hung over from her night before. In the back of their mind they feel sad that Berta still wants to rebel against the entire world and hopes she will soon grow out of that stage that every teenager goes through. They just hope the bad choices she sometimes makes do not leave an impression she will have to overcome for the rest of her life. They also worry about the friends she keeps and their belief that drugs and getting "high" is the purpose of life.

24.

Obsession

Bob is obsessed with the trip or the water. Every morning, every evening and all day long, it consumes her. She feels driven to return. She talks with R.C. about going back. He is conflicted. He knows Bob, probably better than anyone does and accepts that she is different, to some people even strange, but he also knows she is not loco. Bob has a creative mind that is not recognized by most individuals. They simply do not have the ability to see it and often are uncomfortable with what they do not understand. After many years of marriage R. C. has not only grown to understand Bob, but also knows how to love and respect those special feelings she gets, even if they still sound a bit absurd to him. She is usually right and he trusts that her intentions are always good.

Every morning and every night after work R. C. finds Bob in her think tank brooding over the water and its mysteries. Why does it taste so much better than other water – cleaner and crisper?

Does it truly have a "magical" healing quality or was that only her imagination? And, if it was only her imagination, why did R.C. recover so quickly after drinking tea made from it? Finally, what is there that should or could be done about this?

The intensity he sees in Bob's face is like the intensity of a pro athlete that can only see the action in front or at the moment and not hear or see anything else. R.C. knows this water must be important to her and that this is one of those absurd special feelings Bob experiences.

After a few long talks they almost agree to give it one more try and let Bob go back to the mountains to retrieve more samples of the water.

25.

Prep for Trip Two

By Tuesday R.C. knows Bob is going to win her argument, so after work R. C. stops by to see one of the law firms' clients, a pharmaceutical specialty supply shop.

The owner, Mike Pharm, and R.C. shake hands. After the initial civil niceties, Mark says, "So, R.C., what brings you to my neck of the woods?"   R.C. responds, "Bob is at it again, or should I say still?"   They both laugh. R.C. continues, "Yup, she is up to some of her experiments and needs some glass jugs with glass corks."   Mike says, "I got just the right man for you," and calls over to the one they call the "Jugman."

As Gordon, otherwise known as "Jugman," approaches, Mike's secretary walks out of the office and says, "Mike, your wife is on the phone."   Mike says, "OK," and quickly introduces R.C. to Gordy telling Gordy to, "Take good care of R.C. and give him the max on discount."   Mike walks toward his office as Gordon and R.C. shake hands. Gordy asks, "What can I get for you?"

R.C. has learned from Bob some of the dimensions she has to stay under. He tells Gordy he wants the biggest bottles that have a glass cork. Gordy starts to laugh and R.C. looks at him, quizzically. Gordy lets R.C. in on the joke explaining that the cork, as R.C. called it, is really called something else and a word Gordy could neither spell nor pronounce. They both laugh. Gordy said to R.C., "You should have been here the first time I tried to pronounce it," and more laughter erupted.

The total height can only be 9 inches. R.C. thinks she may need a glass funnel on top of the jar as part of the over all height. Gordy pauses and says, "Okay, how about round or square?" R.C. thinks for a moment and says, "That shouldn't make any difference." Gordy takes R.C. back through aisle #3 where they see what R.C. later recalls thinking as "7 million glass jugs."

Gordy walks over to one sample crate that is about 7" high and tells R.C. to wait where he is for a second. Two aisles down Gordy grabs a small funnel and returns asking, "How about this combo?"

R.C. pauses and then exclaims, "Yes, that's it! What took you so long?" They both laugh. The jugs are about 8" by 8" square with a short neck and the glass cork stopper. R.C carries the funnel and Gordy places two cases of the jugs on a cart, rolls them up front and begins to fill out the paperwork.

Standing near Mike's office, R.C. and Gordy chat for a few seconds and shake hands. R.C. waves goodbye to Mike who is still on the phone. Mike waves back.

So now whatever this water is or is not, it will not become compromised or contaminated by any residual chemicals from inside the mason jars Bob had used on her first trip.

26.

Thursday Night

By Tuesday night Bob begin to plead her case to R.C. pounding her fist on the table and saying, "I must go back to the mountains. Please don't get angry with me. It may sound crazy but you know how I am when I get one of those special feelings and this is one of those times. You must have to understand." Little does Bob know that R.C. is ready not just with love and understanding, but also with the jugs and cork stoppers. She runs into his arms, throwing hers around his neck and laughing whispers in his ear, "I absolutely adore you." R.C. hugs his exuberant wife and asks that she not leave until Friday afternoon even though he is not certain she will wait that long.

Thursday evening comes and after a quiet dinner for just the two of them "Wish'n and Hoping" by Dusty Springfield plays on the radio as they wash dishes together. Bob whispers, "R.C.?" He pretends not to hear her. She says it again a little louder, "Hmm?"

"R.C., Honey, " Bob begins to say. R.C. interrupts her with a grin and puts his hand gently over Bob's mouth. He stands up, takes her by the hand and walks her out of the dinning room, the music, "Love is a Many Splendored Thing" emanates throughout the house as they walk down the hall and out to the garage.

Just outside the kitchen/hallway door is a strange tarp covering some boxes. R.C. says, "I know you're going to want to go back, and am I going to win the argument? No, so here." He lets go of Bob's hand and uncovers the boxes explaining, as if she needed any explanation, "Two cases of pharmaceutical glass jugs and glass corks with a glass funnel." Bob is, for the first time, speechless while tears of joy run down her face and her eyes sparkle with love as she gazes at R.C.

Almost in total silence, the two of them work together that night and load the Bronco. For a moment she stands there and wonders how he knew. Even though he can't drive a small nail in straight she knows he has the knowledge, wisdom and understanding that she can only see through his eyes. It may be true that he really does know her better than anyone else, she muses. Certainly, he loves her more than she has ever been loved.

The two of them have almost everything ready for Friday's trip.

27.

Future Plans

Before 8:00 a.m., Rob and Charlotte drop by to talk to Bob about some future plans that Rob and Bob now must rescheduled again for next week when the young people learn that Bob is going back to the mountains.

Rob is furious and thinks Bob is being terribly self-centered. He walks out of the house, fuming and yells, "That's it, I'm never coming back! Another broken promise! You have always been full of empty air. Well, this is the last time the bubble is burst by you or any of you."

R.C. and Bob look at each other. While they don't want to hurt his feelings, they must find out all they can about this water and, in all honesty, it is time Rob begins to assume some responsibility for his life. He has a girlfriend and Bob and R.C. simply cannot always be there for him.

Friday afternoon R.C. has a slow day. He stops by the travel agency to see Bob before she leaves as a surprise.

They talk like the loving couple they are. From the Bronco radio we hear "You light up my life" by Debbie Boone as he holds her in his arms and urges her to promise to be careful - of everything. In their minds they are hoping the questions of this water will be answered on this trip, yet some how they know it is only the beginning of a wild and crazy adventure.

Bob had told R.C. about the noises and they agree that she is to be careful and always pack her pistol at her side. He knows Barney and Betty will be there for her but they are just moral support and not much real help except in Bob's mind. Maybe they give her confidence. Maybe talking to them helps her calm down so that she can better evaluate a situation. Whatever it is, R.C. looks to Barney and Betty and says, "You two take care of our girl, you hear?" They nod.

28.

Back To
The "Funny Water"

Upon her arrival at the site Bob notices what appear to be tracks and other changes, as if someone else had been there. While setting up camp she feels like she is being watched.

Hikers would have to park on the road that she came in on and hike through the heavy wooded area just to be able to see the site. The same goes for the bank on the other side of the small river. Hiking from out side of the area would take two days just to get near the site. She is so far out of town and away from any farms that she just shakes her head at herself and believes the excitement is creating sounds in her mind.

Unknown to her, the mountain man is watching and wondering why she is back and, more importantly, concerned about what to do with or to her.

Strange as it is he seems, he has a soft spot in his heart for her, even though her target practice last time was just inches away from his head. Still, he remembers her drinking the water and the most odiferous aroma from her as a result of it. Ahhh, what memories!

With the glass funnel, Bob begins the process of collecting the water into the glass jugs. By her calculations, given the current flow rate, it should take about nine hours to fill a gallon.

"There will be no target practice this time," Bob says under her breath as she studies the area around the dripping water. It seems to be dripping faster from a flat rock with an odd shinny finish that is mostly covered by other shinny rocks. Not wanting to disturb the area she just studies it like a scientist.

While setting up camp and fixing dinner she decides not to drink any of the Water. She would rather take as much back as possible. Eventually, she gives in remembering how clean and crisp it tasted. She toasts the trip with a few drops.

The trip goes well and in just a few days she even ventures upstream where she found an area ideal for target shooting. There are plenty of leaves and dead trees at her favorite range of about 150 to 175 yards away.

Bob found trees that seem to be cut in a way that would make them fall across the stream and create a makeshift bridge. "A clever beaver or maybe someone with a ax," she surmised, "must have built this. Whatever animal or man, it almost looks like tracks." The hair on the back of her neck bristles as she calls out, "Does someone live out here?" Oh, yes the mountain man is watching, as always, just watching.

The mountain man's world is being invaded, not just by this woman but by someone and it seems to be on somewhat of a regular basis.

Bob fills up her last jug with the funny water. It is time to go home and back to work.

Wistfully, she begins to break camp. Bob doesn't regret the return trip. It is just there are still unanswered questions and she wishes she could stay longer. She hates going back to civilization without knowing all the answers and seriously doubts that R.C. would understand yet a third trip.

There are still so many questions, about the water mostly, and now the feeling of being watched and the trees made into a bridge and the flat area where she fills the jugs. As her mind races through all of the imponderables, even more of the hair on her neck stands up.

The peace and tranquility of this area seem too good to be true.

Taking a deep breath she reassures herself that this is real, and not just some episode of "Disney's Wonder Full World of Mountains."

As she packs the Bronco, she still hears sounds of someone or something from behind the wall of trees and bushes that keeps the hair on her neck from settling down.

Her mind is filled with the thought of tranquility and comfort of this beautiful spot and loving nature. Questions appear in her head, "Why do I have to return? Why not just stay here and live off the land in this paradise of complete peace and quiet? Most of all, why hasn't anyone else camped out here and stayed, forever?" Suddenly the wind blows and a limb from a dead tree breaks off falling just inside the tree line next to the Bronco. Bob jumps and swings around looking for someone. Or have they?

She stops and writes a note. The noises make her hair stand up on the back of her neck. Writing seems to calm her nerves, just to address these sounds. She starts off with:

"Hi, Ed. I'm calling you Ed.

I don't know your name

so I've given you a name.

It's a nice name,

with respect and dignity.

I hope you will understand

I'm not here to cause any problems.

Someday I hope to see you.

My name is Roberta, but they call me Bob.

That's it for now, until next time.

I'm not sure if I'm coming back.

So, bye for now!

Your friend, Bob"

29.

Mountain Man's Hide Out

As she drives away from the campsite, a big bearded man picks up the note, smells it and reads it. It smells like her and now he knows her name is Bob. He remembers that while Bob was out hiking and filling bottles, he stopped by her camp. She was far enough away that he could investigate a bit. He goes to the Bronco. The doors are not locked. Why would they be? Obviously she is a trusting soul who is miles from anywhere and hopefully anyone. After all, this is way out in the middle of nowhere. He opens the passenger side door where Barney and Betty sit. Their button eyes look up at him. They start to fall out of the Bronco. His natural reaction is to catch them, and he does. He pauses and slightly, ever so slightly, smiles from under his beard, as if catching Barney and Betty remind him of some memories of things in his past.

He looks around to see if anyone is watching even though this is his town, his mountain, his valley and his neighborhood.

He scans the rest of the Bronco just for the record. Seeing nothing to worry about he carefully puts Barney and Betty in place like a loving couple, closes the door and walks away towards his man-made hut, built into the side of the mountain across the stream and up the hill from the spring. It is on a very steep slope and so well camouflaged to look like part of the mountain that anyone looking for it would just walk by. He raises up an awning of limbs, vines and leaves to get to the entrance, This "door" doubles as a sun roof and looks so natural the birds land on it and the squirrels climb all over it. He props two legs to hold it up. Obviously, the vines and limbs have been woven by a master and appear so natural that only the trees and bushes know the difference.

Inside, on the right we see pictures of a family, a tall, handsome and smooth shaven man with a beautiful wife and two young sons. This is on the mantel over his small fireplace.

Under this mountain man's bearded face is this same man, as in the picture. Only the mountain man has grown a beard and where there once was a brilliant gleam in his eyes and happy countenance, the bearded man's eyes show great pain and his face a profound sadness and despair. Why would a man leave such a nice looking family to live out here? What has he done or to whom? Or, what has happened to him?

Besides the fireplace with mantel, the hut is equipped with a cot, a large chair, a small table for eating, all beautifully hand made, and a library of many books. Above the bookshelf is a gun rack with a military style rifle and boxes of shells. Off to the left we see him open a cabinet that reveals a pantry full of can goods: soups, meats, canned fruits and a major assortment of MRE's (military for Meals Ready to Eat). It appears to be enough food for a few months.

The inside of his hut is meticulously clean and neat. Everything has a place and nothing is out of its place. Next to the pantry is the front of a chrome and black Harley Davidson motorcycle, in mint condition, aiming out from a tunnel dug into the side of the mountain, and all neatly boarded around the bike for easy exit. It appears this is his mode of transportation or method of "get away"?

30.

Burn

After the normal five hours of driving Bob just wants to unload and rest. She pulls into her Beacon Crest Circle driveway, walks to the back and opens the Bronco just as she hears screams of pain from the neighbors' house. She hurries over to their back yard from where the sounds are coming just in time to see their little girl running to the house with burns all over her left arm and hand. The charcoal grill is on its side and it looks like little Jane, the little girl, fell into the burning coals.

Alice, her mother, comes running out of the house at the same time. Both ladies make her lie down and roll her in the ground to extinguish the burning.

Little Jane is still crying in pain. Her dark blue eyes are filled with giant tears running down her cheek and her beautiful red hair is flying all over as she turns her head back and forth in both pain and fear.

Bob quickly grabs the garden hose, turns on the water to a fine spray. Alice holds Janey's arm and helps Bob spray some of the cool water in an effort to see how badly the arm is burnt.

After cooling down the arm and hand and cleaning the charcoal off the arm they know it's bad. Little Jane is still crying from pain. "Alice, I don't want to frighten Janey, but I think you really should take her to the hospital. At least they might be able to reduce the scarring," Bob suggests. Alice agrees and goes into the house to get the keys for the car as Bob, comforting as best she can, takes Jane out to the driveway.

As she walks toward the Bronco, Bob then wonders about the "funny water" and runs over to the Bronco, just a few feet away, and grabs a bottle. Thinking they can take it along to the hospital to keep Jane's arm cool, pours some on Jane's arm and hand.

As Bob pours it on Jane's arm and hand Alice, with concern on her face, comes out of the house. She looks at Bob and, being a good friend of Bob's, knows she would never do anything to hurt Jane so she does not ask any questions about this mysterious jug of water.

They watch the foaming and bubbling of the water, as if it were hydrogen peroxide. Jane stops crying and watches. She says, "Mommy it feels cool, it's not burning any more, Mommy."

Other neighbors join in to help and they too are amazed at what has just happened. As the foaming action slows down Bob pours more water from the bottle over the area and washes off her arm. Jane says, "Mommy it feels good." The arm is still a dark cherry red but looks like it has started healing.

One of the other neighbors, Grace, a nurse, speaks up and wants to go to the hospital with Alice and Jane. Everybody looks at each other as to say "Well, yea, It's nurse Grace, why not?" Alice quickly reply's "Oh yes, thank you."

31.

To The Hospital

Everyone helps load the three into the red Windstar mini van. Alice looks to Bob and says, "Aren't you coming along?" She knows Grace, but Grace is more Bob's friend and although Alice trusts her, she wants her undivided attention on Janey. "No, you'll be just fine and I still have my unpacking to do," explains Bob.

On the way Grace knows the safety rules and instructs Alice to turn on the headlights and emergency flashers. At each intersection she pulls up and blows her horn to tell other drivers she will be going next and proceed with caution. They have to do this three times and other drivers seem to know something has happened and back off for the few seconds needed. Alice and Grace wave to them as a "thank you."

At the hospital, Alice, Jane and Grace arrive and quickly take Jane into the emergency room. Nurse Grace knows all the doctors and other nurses. She greets everyone then with the speed of a good nurse tells the attending physician about Jane's collision with the charcoal grill and her burns on the arm and hand. Alice stands back knowing Grace is not only a good nurse, but also a very good friend. Grace can deal with the doctors as Alice is taken to a counter where she can do all the paperwork.

By this time more of the redness has faded from Jane's arm and hand. After taking all of Jane's vitals and with the help of two other nurses, the Doctor is wondering why Jane is even in the emergency room. The burns seem to be just superficial and only need some ointment to ward off any possible infection.

He turns to Grace with more questions about the accident. Grace is just as confused and really doesn't have any good answers. Grace tells the Doctor of the water Bob poured over the arm and hand explaining that it foamed up and that Jane said it felt cool and stopped hurting.

The Doctor being a friend of Bob's and the Ebner family asks Grace to have Bob give him a call. Grace, Alice and the happy little patient Jane soon pack up and head for home.

Bob is in a state of disbelief at what she just saw. When they arrive back home, some of the neighbors ask Bob what was in the water she has no clear answer. She stutters and can only say, "It was just some real clean distilled water," and quickly changes the subject continuing her unpacking and never really looking her neighbors in the face.

32.

R. C. Comes Home

R.C. arrives home to find Bob in the garage unpacking and staring out the window of her think tank. She tries to tell R.C. about the burn and the water but doesn't know where to start. At the same time she has a thousand questions about the water herself.

"R. C., little Jane dumped over their grill and fell into the coals," Bob begins. R.C. starts to say something. Bob places her hand gently over his mouth. "You've got to hear this. I grabbed one of the bottles of this funny water and poured it over the burns," she continued, pausing and taking a deep breath. Still holding her hand on R.C., "It foamed up but Jane said it felt cool," Bob takes another breath, "There's more. I poured it on again and it washed the arm clean. It seems to have started healing the burns." She takes her hand down with another breath.

R.C. is speechless for a moment. "Okay, dear what are your thoughts about what happened, your first thought?"

R.C. pauses then says again, "Remember Bob just your first thoughts," with the voice of a trial lawyer or judge.

Bob chokes and then with a quivering voice finally says, "I knew the water was cold and thought that alone could make it feel good on Jane's arm, but I did not expect the foaming or the pain to go away. I am surprised and now a bit perplexed. The water tasted good and tested clear. I just don't understand," she says with a far-away look in her eyes. Then suddenly focuses on R.C. and says raising her eyebrows and smiling, "And you know how I hate to not know."

R.C. grabs her shoulders, looks into her eye's with the big question mark on his face almost afraid to ask, "And then?"

Bob walks to shelves where she had placed the jugs of water, grabs one and says, "We all watched for a moment and I poured more water on it to wash the foam away. It washed it away all right and with it, the water seemed to wash away the burn. Seriously! The arm wasn't as red and seemed to be healing already. Little Jane was happy and smiling. I swear all I used was water from this jug. That's when Grace said she would go with Alice to the hospital, we all helped them get loaded and they left."

Bob, as animated as R.C. had ever seen her, continued to explain to him that she believed there was something different about the water. "Did you ever wonder why I went camping leaving you when we were all just coming down with the flu yet when I returned I was "fit as a fiddle" and you were still "sicker than a dog? Well, it must have been the water. I drank it, after I tested it, of course, while I was camping. Then, when I got home and saw how sick you still were, you poor handsome fellow, I made some tea with it. After a couple of sips you were well enough to, well, get frisky. Remember?" Bob winks. "What I don't understand is how the same water can help with the flu bug and also with burns. If it bubbles in our stomachs the way it bubbled on Jane's arm and hand, no wonder we had some really smelly you know what," Bob muses.

Grace calls from the car on her cell phone and tells Bob that she, Alice and Jane are on their way home and that the doctor would like to have Bob call him. All he did was give Alice some ointment and said it looked great. And than she asks "What is in that water?" Bob can only say that it was some clean distilled water. She couldn't tell Grace anything because she simply did not know.

Bob starts making more trips to get more samples, to test more friends, to test more burns and flu. The list goes on and on and the time spent by Bob also goes on and on. She becomes obsessed with this water. Soon the business is failing. Her one remaining employee, Fran, can only do so much.

Bob tries to help when she is in town, but it seems that the more Bob tests the water, the greater the number of questions. All of her basic chemistry tests indicate that this is simple H20, water. Bob even tests the spring's production knowing that the spring only can fill one gallon in nine hours, maybe she can "cultivate" more in her think tank. Nothing seems to work.

Time and time again, BOB finds excuses to reschedule business plans or meetings with friends so that she can surreptitiously make a day trip to the mountains or conclude some experiment. She isn't sleeping. Rob is so fed up that every time he comes over resolved to make amends with Bob, after changing his plans to fit with her schedule, he ends up walking out because something more important, the water, had Bob's full attention. Each time he vows, "OK, that's it, Good by forever!" A few days later,

Bob calls Rob, apologizes and reschedules. Then, the same pattern repeats itself. The water . . . always the water.

33.

Notes For Ed

People from town who have long been Bob's clients, walk past the storefront of the travel agency and peer in to see the store is vacant. The owner of the property has had a "Three Day Notice to Quit or Pay" sign posted to the door for more than a week. He has known Bob for such a long time that he is not really about to commence an eviction proceeding and is more concerned about her health than the past due rent that is owed. Still, business is business.

Grace talks to the doctors about Bob. They suggest she is not hardwired completely and suggest Grace give Bob some space and stay away.

Each time Bob returns to the woods and mountains for more water, she hears more noises in the woods. "Am I truly crazy and just hearing things or about to suffer some psychotic break, or is there really someone out there?" Bob, in a more lucid moment, questions Barney and Betty. They nod but she is not certain to which part of the question they agree. Bob begins to leave more notes, always placing them in or around the same place. "Curious that I never see any remnants of my notes. I wonder if a squirrel or bird carry them away to add to their nests or if someone is actually reading them. No, can't be," she half-mutters to herself. And so, she writes:

------------ NOTES TO ED -------------

Ed,

I hope everything is all right with you.

The water from this spring seemed to

cure a flu bug my husband and I had.

At least I think it is the water. It is all

I can think that might be possible.

The water has also done some other

strange things, but they are too

complicated to tell you. Just be careful

of the water.

Your friend,

Bob

Ed,

I not sure if the animals are eating the notes or not or if you even exist. Just in case you do, here are some crackers, candy and canned foods that I have left from the many trips.

Please enjoy them, you have been

A good friend, even though we

have not met.

Your friend,

Bob

Strange as it seems when Bob returns to the same spot on her next trip, the crackers are gone without a trace. Although the candy and canned food is also missing, the wrappers of both are left behind. "This is really weird," Bob thinks to herself, "I wonder what animal would take the label from a can of Campbell's tomato soup. I can see eating the Snickers here and leaving the wrapper, but why the wrapper of the soup? Very odd!"

In the evenings, after dark when the campsite is quiet and the camp light only goes so far, that is when Bob sits down and writes her notes. She stares at the moon and stars as she pens her notes. The notes Bob writes have feelings of passion, gratitude and friendship in them even though a deer maybe eating them.

Bob's humming of the tune "Is that all there Is" by Peggy Lee strangely echoes across the stream to the ears of the mountain man and a smile nearly appears under his beard as if he feels the warmth of the tune. Some nights the Mountain Man sits across the stream just watching her and just wonders what she is doing and why.

34.

Testing

Unknown to Bob, friends secretly help test this funny water on themselves and other friends at the hospital, drug clinics and burn treatment centers.

One of the doctors hears of this and becomes concerned that someone may be practicing medicine without a license. The buzz around the hospital increases in magnitude until finally one of doctors contacts the police department and starts a problem. He sits down with the police chief and tells his one sided story to the man who can and will make things worse.

The Doctor does what he can from the medical side and the chief puts out the word to keep people away from the Ebner's. He privately encourages anyone to make things difficult for them, as he starts to do it anyway the police can. The police begin to stop family members for, at most, insignificant offenses.

Generally there is no violation at all like the time Rob and Charlotte were stopped because Rob failed to turn on his emergency flashers when he stopped in front of the drugstore to drop off Charlotte. The stop took all of ten seconds.

Or, the time R.C. was stopped at a stop sign, looked in all four directions and noticed the police patrol car half-hidden on one of the side roads. The officer was clearly looking down. Just as R.C. entered the intersection, the officer looked up and, having not seen R.C. prior to that instance, believed R.C. had not stopped for the posted sign. Each stop was annoying and required time from an otherwise busy schedule to deal with what had become a problem.

The local police chief is an ex-lover of Angel's. Back in their college days Angel made the decision to marry the chief's best friend when all three ran around together. After twenty years of a great marriage to her husband, John Summit died of cancer.

The Chief was so upset when Angel chose his buddy John over him that he never spoke to them again. But, deep down he knew that Angel and John were his best friends. They always remembered him during the holidays, birthdays, and his promotions as well as the low times in his life like the death of his mother. Always, they remembered. The Chief didn't go to John's funeral, but had the funeral director privately let him in to pay his last respects after calling hours. The director was also a friend to Angel and called her later that night. She felt the warmth of the situation and kept it to herself.

35.

Secret Leaks Out

The secret of the water begins to leak out to the community. All of a sudden news reporters hound and embarrass the family. Traffic outside the Beacon Crest home is so thick that neighbors are upset with the Ebners and mostly blame Bob.

Rob blows up about his nutty Mother. R.C gets a warning from the law firm and Berta and her friends find it a good reason to turn to more drugs, as if they required a reason.

News of the water even travels back east through the Internet and some, more than others, are over interested. Some look at it as the "Gold Rush" of the 1800's and want to get the secret at any cost. Others start moving to Vallivue Falls in hopes of finding the secret. It seems that each day there are moving vans and trucks heaped with personal belongings lining the major traffic arteries of Vallivue Falls. The once peaceful village has become a nightmare and Bob's neighbors, friends and family blame her.

People start to follow everyone in the family and spy on the house. Cars drive around the circle in front of the house late at night, blow their horns and quickly drive away not knowing that the police have been told to stay away. Even though the police do nothing to intervene, there seems to be a patrol car and police vehicles parked in places where they can see the house and everything that goes on from any direction. This alarms some of the neighbors – those same neighbors and friends who attended the annual Easter Egg party and, it goes without saying, that it crimps Berta's lifestyle.

Rob and his Charlotte, who do not even live at the Beacon Crest address, have their own special pair of shadows. No one seems to know who they are.

The travel business has more problems. A few of the longstanding clients fear that while they are on their trip the travel agency will go under. Others express concern that their deposit money for the "trip of a lifetime" may be used to finance another personal excursion for Bob for more of this "funny water."

Fran, the one remaining staff member, cannot get into the storefront through the throngs of inquisitive onlookers who wait hoping to catch a glimpse of Bob.

Finally, one day after lunch, Fran gives up. She returns to her car and, calling Bob with her cell phone says, "Sorry, Lady. I can't do this anymore. The clients I was helping I will try to finish from home. I just can't get into the office."

"I understand, Fran," replies Bob.

"No, you don't – you really truly don't. You haven't been here for a month or nearly that. I love you like a sister and so I say this out of love. You have to give this up, Bob. It is ruining your life and that of your family's. I will try to make it back to the office tonight, after dinner, to retrieve the computer and all important documents. I'll work from my home to the best of my ability. Oh, and by the way, you owe me for not only my salary but for the back rent," Fran explains with loving concern in her voice.

"Back rent? Oh, no, I forgot all about that. Oh, Fran, I guess you are right and I will stop this insanity soon, I promise, only right now," Bob says in an attempt to placate Fran.

"I know, honey. I know you. Once you get your teeth into a problem, you just can't let it go. Only promise me you will stick your head up once in a while for some fresh air. And, don't worry about the money. I'm pretty flush at the moment. I love you. You take care, sweetie," Fran capitulates hanging up the phone.

36.

Being Followed

BOB makes the decision that with R.C.'s practice dwindling and her travel agency business closing except for what Fran is able to do from home, she has no choice but to sell some funny water to some rich neighbors. Other trips and more research must be conducted and she is running out of capital. Her friend, Ken Smith and his wife, help. They arrange for Bob to meet other affluent individuals who may be of assistance to the cause, so long as they can see it as a cause and thereby stroking their egos.

Ken and his wife also arrange for Bob to meet people in large truck stops off the freeway, in parking lots, in back of school yards, anyplace that is open and there is certainty no police are around, for the individuals to buy funny water. Even to an independent, untrained observer, it is not hard to figure out that Bob is selling more water just to survive. Bob feels and even acts more and more like a drug smuggler.

37.

Discovery of Gold

On one of the trips to the spring BOB discovers the water flows through what appears to be seven layers of a gold nuggets that are thin and the size of a skate boards. The water drips off the end. "WOW, riches or the water!" Bob exclaims. "I wonder why I didn't notice that before? Oh, yes, now I remember, the first time I was here I was sick with the flu and, now that I look around, I guess I have traveled a bit further than I have been before." Barney and Betty nod.

Lying awake half of the night she hears all sorts of noises including her animal friends walking around in the woods.

The mountain man has no idea what troubles she has in town. Still, each time she comes to camp, after she has obviously gone to sleep, he snoops around to see if she brought anyone along. Seeing no one he goes off to his own house.

Thinking about the gold Bob had discovered, she begins to consider the riches it would bring to her and the family. She stares into the stars dreaming of how much easier it would make things financially.

At bedtime, on the second night after the discovery, she cannot sleep thinking about the gold. If she came home with the gold and no water it would end all the harassment. It would end the laughter and finger pointing and relieve pressure at R.C.'s office. Rob would be happy and they could do some things together again she has long promised him. Berta would stop worrying and hopefully stay away from more drugs.

But what about all the good things the water has already done and what it can still do. Maybe the gold adds something to the water that, although imperceptible, changes the water to have the funny qualities. If she removed the gold would the water still be "funny?" Or, would taking the money just be selfish? That's not Bob. She remembers little Jane's burns and how it worked. She remembers the flu bug that she and R.C. had and the cure.

She stands looking out over the stream into the full moon sky And says first to herself, "No." Then looks up again and says louder, "No, I can't give up." Her eyes well up with tears and her legs crumble under her body as she sits down on the grassy weeds. Her head falls down in her hands with deep thought and her eyes run with tears.

Across the stream Mountain Man Ed stands in the shadows, his .357 drawn, looking for someone to whom Bob is speaking. Is he a friend or foe of Bob? Is this water his secret? He wonders what she is talking about. What is she not "giving up?" With an audible, "Harrumph, Mountain Man wonders why he even cares. Even though Bob has been a "tidy neighbor," his paradise is disturbed and his daily routine requires adjustment every time she visits the mountain. His hospitality is wearing thin as he is close to having had enough of Bob. Maybe he should make certain she never comes back.

38.

Rob And Char Break Up

Bob no sooner gets home than Rob and Charlotte pull into the driveway. "Mom, for love of God and your family, you've got to stop this insanity! We don't see you anymore and when we do you are too tired to talk. Do you even recognize yourself in the mirror? Please, stop. You just have to or I, no we simply cannot continue to stop by. We won't be pushed aside by this obsession with this stupid funny water. We've had it. We all have," Rob urges with love and also disgust in his voice.

"Wait a minute, Rob. Don't you be speakin' for me. Who do you think you are tellin' your Mom what to do? If she's gotta dream, she's gotta dream," Charlotte says siding with Bob. Bob half smiles as if she needed Charlotte's approval.

"Who do I think I am? Who do I think I am? I'm her son, for Christ's sake! Don't you dare take sides against me with my family! You have no friggin' idea what she has put us through – what she is putting herself through," Rob screams at Charlotte.

Bob goes off to her think tank leaving the two of them to squabble at each other, puts her head in her hands and cries. This water is taking its toll and breaking up the family.

Charlotte moves back to a dorm room at college. Both Rob and Charlotte spend the evenings in their own little separate worlds, looking at walls and missing the love they truly had.

Rob, in an act of both desperation and rebellion begins to date one of Berta's newest drug friends. This girl, Vickie, is very attractive and although Berta sometimes thinks she has more on her shoulders than her other friends and may be some form of plant, the girl certainly can party. Although Berta and Rob don't know it, Vickie is a very expensive out-of-state call girl who has the threat of a lengthy bust hanging over her head. Her pending time as an inmate is resting on how much she can learn about the water and Rob's movements.

His family in crises, R.C. asks for and takes temporary leave from the law firm. All of his cases are transferred to other partners so that he and Bob have some long talks.

"Bob, I know how preoccupied you are with this project of yours and so I almost hate to burden you with something so mundane is a family matter – not that you truly care about anything or anyone else anymore, but I'm really worried about Berta," begins R.C. "She never gets out of bed until around 4:00 in the afternoon. Then she is out by 10:00 and who knows what time she gets in – probably sometime after the bars close. As far as I can tell, she hasn't eaten a healthy meal in a few weeks and she is losing a lot of weight. Even the dark circles under her eyes have circles. I've been thinking about it. I've taken a short leave from the firm and am taking her out of town to visit my cousins. The hundred miles or so might just be enough of a distance from her friends to help her on the path to recovery. And, if that doesn't work, we are going to have to put her through a rehab course. It's just that those programs are really expensive and between my taking a leave and your business going under, we can't swing that kind of expenditure right now," R.C. continues.

Berta, who slowly descends from upstairs holding herself up by the banister as she goes, overhears her dad and mom talking and is livid.

"Well, R.C., if that is what you think is best," Bob responds as if in her own little dream world. R.C. is right. Of course Berta needs help. Even Bob recognizes that, but she just does not have the time, let alone the energy, to cope with any other issue and is thankful to R.C. for taking the lead on this one.

Meanwhile, Rob and Charlotte text each other and want to talk. Rob and Char get together with out the new friend Vickie knowing. They arrange for Rob to drive by the dorm and pick Charlotte up with plans to drive to the park in town and talk.

39.

The Kidnapping

Alex Mooruny from New York insists his newly hired thugs call him "Big Al," and since he is only 5' tall, no one better snicker in doing so.

Big Al is one of the many that have heard about special water. He thinks he can make a name for himself with the "big" guys by getting the secret to the water. He had all the family followed and he even got Vicki, the young hooker, to become friends with Berta so she could get closer to Rob. Little does Big Al know that Vicki is already tailing Rob on behalf of the police in the hope that her cooperation will reduce her sentence on a series of charges. Vickie's rap sheet is almost as long as she is tall – such a shame for such a great looking gal.

Rob and Char, after a series of long text messages and telephone calls, are back together, however the bond is still a bit tenuous and with lots of tears and small hugs. Small fights still erupt with the two in total disagreements about Bob and her trips to the mountain and spring for the water.

Vickie carefully watches for every advantage to step in. It all started one evening when Rob was over at her Berta's dorm room. Vickie faked car problems just to get Rob to help start her car. After the car starts she thanks Rob by taking him out for dinner at a local restaurant she can afford. All during the meal, Vickie pretends to be attentive and interested in everything Rob has to say, praising him with eyes wide open. Rob has been missing that attention, particularly since he has not been able to speak to his mom.

Dinner eventually leads to a hug and a kiss followed by small talk and more kisses and more.

40.

Shoot Out Time

A warehouse in the industrial area of town is being rented by a little, short, runt of a man for his dirty work. In the back of the building, on the north side, is a hill where part of the building foundation was dug out of the side of the hill. The hill tapers up about 8' and is topped off by weeds and bushes.

Bob and Tiny hide in the weeds and peer through the dirty windows. Through the brown streaks, they can barely make out the image of two hooded people. Bob stares intently for some clue as to who the two people are. Then, it comes to her. Based on their attire, which she can barely see, she knows the two are Rob and Charlotte. "Looks like four nasty lookin' men in there with them, Ma'am," says Tiny. "Suredoes," Bob agrees. "It seems like that little runt of a man is in command. It sounds like he has a real Napoleonic complex. Guess he demands the three call him

"Big Al. Yeah, right," continues Bob, her voice trembling with nervousness.

On the south side of the building is another empty warehouse with a fire ladder going up the backside. Bob and Tiny climb up and look over the edge. They can see the same view of Rob and Charlotte from the other side of the building with Big Al and his band of ugly thugs.

With walkie-talkies and inventions from her think tank, Bob orchestrates what might be taken for a shoot-out from the opposite sides of the factory. At least she and Tiny hope that the captors will believe that the building is surrounded.

Bob looks through the windows and sees the side of Al Mooruny's head. Looking down at the table she sees pistols in the hands of the ugly thugs. "People like that don't deserve ordinances," laments Bob. "Ma'am?" Tiny questions. Bob, looking into Tiny's eyes replies, "Guns can be truly beautiful and should be respected. Stupid people do stupid things like waving them around. That's when people get hurt. It isn't the guns that kill, it is stupidity that kills." Tiny returns her gaze understanding that they are of kindred spirit when it comes to weapons. Clearly, Big Mama did not understand that this little lady had some big time training somewhere in her life. Tiny immediately understands that Bob is in control and he is there only for support and to cover her flank if need be.

After a while, the three place the pistols on the table between the hooded Rob and Charlotte.

Bob and Tiny quietly walk to the back of the building, climb down the ladder and return to the north side of the building. This is the side that has the most weeds, natural camouflage material.

On their way, Bob goes around the backside of the building while Tiny travels around the front for a full survey of all the windows and doors. By the time Tiny travels the longer route Bob has already set up a tri-pod to hold one of her rifles aimed at one pistol on the table. Bob carefully wires the rifle's trigger mechanism to a remote control device that will fire it when she pushes a button. She has designed this little trigger devise from a garage door opener.

As she turns around to go to the south side of the building she raises up and bumps Tiny. Tiny has been leaning over her shoulders and watching just an inch away. He smiles and says, "After we set up the speakers, I'll stay here with this set-up and a walkie-talkie just to make sure nothing moves it."

Bob's forehead is at his chin and all she can say as she looks up at his smile is a quivering, "Okay." Tiny gently grabs her arm and says, "You can do this, Ma'am. You've been trained and so have I. We can do this." Bob is only slightly reassured after all, it is her kids, not his.

They both climb down the hillside and set up four wireless speakers in the bushes. This is Bob's setup from the back yard Easter party that Ken Smith uses for all the announcements. Tiny than heads back to the hillside and weeds while Bob goes to the Bronco and turns on the controls for the wireless speakers and the wireless microphone that she puts in her pocket.

Big Al leaves the factory in the old rusty green van. Bob and Tiny are still setting up all of the equipment as he drives away. The element of surprise is one that cannot be underestimated, so Bob and Tiny move very quietly from opposite sides of the factory. Although she wants the kids to know she is there, she certainly does not want to be fully seen.

From the walkie-talkie, Bob asks Tiny if everything is in place. "A, Okay," he responds. Bob pulls the wireless microphone out of her pocket, flips the switch and announces, "This is the Vallivue Falls police SWAT Team. The building is surrounded." As she makes the announcement, one of the Uglys reaches for a gun. Bob pushes the button on the rigged garage door opener at the same time she fires with the rifle in her arms, convincing them there is a whole SWAT team. One of the three Uglys is grazed in the arm of the hand that grabbed the gun. She announces again and they all quickly raise their arms.

She furiously climbs down the fire ladder and runs over to the door with her pistol drawn only to find Tiny waiting for her. He opens the big door and they both go in. The ugly thugs are waiting for more of a SWAT team then just little Bob and start to think that they can over power this beautiful lady until they hear a loud. "I wouldn't do that if I were you," coming from the shadows. They get a good look at Tiny as he walks closer to them and says "Gentlemen, do what the lady says, hands UP". Their arms stand up real straight at that point.

She and Tiny rescue the kids, handcuff all three of the thugs together and call the police. As the police arrive Tiny disappears.

The call Bob made was to the police 911 center. She stated that she just had a shoot-out with the kidnappers of Rob and Charlotte and needed some assistance in taking the kidnappers in to the police station and one had been injured.

This embarrassed the police Chief. Three police cars arrive in seconds with guns drawn, Tiny had left the large door open so they can see in. They see Bob, Rob and

Charlotte standing next to three ugly men, holding them at gunpoint.

The next car that arrives is the Chief and he is furious.

The Chief has Bob arrested for City Code firearm violation of discharging a firearm in city limits and attempted murder of the injured man. He has all taken to the police station. The injured man and the kids go straight to the hospital in the back of two police cruisers.

Bob is taken in a separate cruiser. The Chief reads Bob her rights. He wants no mistake being made about this one. Normally his officers attempt to talk to an arrestee to get a statement from them. Not in this case. The Chief is so furious that he won't even talk to her. "How is it going to look to the Commissioner when he learns that Bob, this small headstrong woman did his job saving Rob and Charlotte?" he mumbles to himself.

Bob is fingerprinted and photographed, being charged with firearms violations and for attempted murder of the injured man. Bob is taken into an interrogation room and sits down with one of the other Officers. She gives a statement about the kidnapping and rescue but carefully omits all reference to Tiny or Big Mama, as well as any detail of how she was able to accomplish the rescue. There is no need for the police to know about the special training Col. Max arranged for her to go to receive. To keep her mind focused, Bob concentrates on the indignity of being arrested on these petty charges. She is furious at the Police Chief for having her arrested. When asked by the officer for more information she says nothing. Bob knows to wait for R.C. to come back in town and guide her with his legal knowledge in the right direction. She exercises her Miranda rights and states, "That is it until I have an attorney present."

Bob takes this as a stand-off of major powers like the World War II, Patton –v- Rommal classic and this is just part of her "Water Storm." As Col. Max taught her, "When you're right, stand up and say so, if you're not sure, keep shut." Although Bob knows she is right, she also knows better than to stand up without her attorney. After all, she is most likely better trained than any rookie cop.

41.

Virus At The Hospital

Although Rob and Char insisted they were fine, Bob was adamant that they should go to the hospital for a check up. The only injuries seem to be an injection given by the thugs. Several vials of blood were taken from each so the lab could perform a full panoply of tests. "We won't have the full results from the lab for a day or two, but of two things we are certain. All three of you have been infected by some form of low grade virus although you don't seem to have a fever," began the doctor.

"All three?" Rob questions looking around the room and seeing that only he and Charlotte are there. "You mean both of us, don't you? Or, is my mom infected too?"

"No, no I meant all three. You didn't let me finish. Charlotte, do you want me to tell Rob or shall I," continues the doctor. Char is speechless. Of course she knows exactly what the doctor is saying but hasn't told Rob. Not wanting to see face for fear he will be panic, she starts sobbing and hyperventilating. The doctor quickly steps in, calms her down, and, smiling at Rob says, "Congratulations! You are going to be a Dad!"

There are no other affects at present. Until the lab work comes back, the Doctor saw no reason to keep the kids and sends them home.

Some of the police grew up with Rob. Regardless of what the Chief says, they want to help Rob and Charlotte. "Say, Rob, we have to give you a ride somewhere. Me and the guys have been thinking that you should probably go to your mom and dad's house. That way the neighbors can all help keep a lookout," says a young police person, quietly so no other officers can hear him. "Yeah, that's right," chimes in the officer's female partner. "Hey, Ro-bo, I can give you two a ride if you can wait about ten minutes. I'll be off duty then," says a third officer who had gone to high school with Rob. "Can you hang until then?" "Sure," says Rob, looking at Charlotte with his arms around her. "A Dad, Huh!"

Preston, the police officer, gives Rob and Charlotte a ride home. Although he and Rob are good friends, Charlotte gets the seat of honor, the passenger seat, with Rob sitting in the back.

Even though Bob rescued them, Rob is still furious with his Mom. Still, he knows Preston and the other police officers are right. They would be safer at his parents' home.

Once they arrive, Rob paces back and forth thinking of what to do and how to handle the situation. Now that he is going to be a Dad, he has to begin to step up to the plate. How dare his mother and her crazy actions place Charlotte in such a predicament?

Charlotte goes to the refrigerator and eyes beautiful square bottles with a glass cork. What else would a Blond do but drink some of the "funny water." Once again, the water has the standard run-to-the-outhouse reaction. She washes her mouth out with some more water and runs back to the bathroom. After this time she feels better, but still a bit funny and asks Rob to take her back to the hospital. One last trip to the bathroom, this time sitting down, the most foul odor Rob and his police buddies have ever smelled wafts its way out of the bathroom. Even the sanitizing spray does nothing to dissipate the aroma. "God, Rob, what does your lady eat?" asks one of the officers. Rob's face turns red as a beat.

"Ro-o-o-o-o-b, I think I need to go back to the hospital," cries Charlotte. By now Rob has heard her cry so many times, he takes his time getting to her. "Okay guys, which of you will let her ride in your car?" His police buddies all look at each other and play a round of "rock, paper, scissors" to determine the loser who has to give Charlotte a ride back to the hospital.

Once at the hospital, the doctor suggests all three have additional blood tests. This time, they are asked to wait in the lounge until the results arrive from the lab. "Unbelievable! It seems that the killer virus in Charlotte and the fetus is all gone. Only Rob is still infected," exclaims the doctor.

Back home Rob listens to his cop buddy and Charlotte convince him to drink some water. "He has nothing to loose," they argue. He drinks some of his mom's "funny water" and after the second and third large gulps, his stomach and intestines begin to erupts just as Charlotte's had. Exactly like Charlotte, and Bob and R.C., although Rob knows nothing of his parents' experience, the fourth trip to the bathroom has such a lethal smell that the odor alone is almost sufficient to render someone unconscious. "Whoa, that sure is some stench!" exclaims Rob as he exists the bathroom feeling a world better.

Rob's cop buddy insists that Rob return for a third time to the hospital. Rob argues, "Hey, Man, I can drive myself." "Yeah, but will you?" Preston questions Rob. They all suggest that Charlotte can stay home this time as Preston and Rob climb back into the police car.

True to form, Rob's blood test this time is clear: no virus. "How can that be?" ask the lab tech and doctors. Officer Preston responds, "It is all under investigation," and quickly pushes Rob out the door.

"Rob, the reason I didn't want Charlotte to come this trip is because we need to talk. For some reason, the higher ups have instructed us to stay clear of you and your family. At the same time, we are ordered to observe you at all times. Do you know what that means?" begins Preston. "Well, no not exactly," confesses Rob. "That means that your mom is into something pretty heavy. It wasn't by accident that you and Charlotte were kidnapped. Those thugs wanted something and we think it has something to do with a project your mom is working on. Anyway, she is risking everything to save your sorry ass. You're my bro, so I can tell you this. You need to grow up, especially now that you are going to be a Dad. You need to be there for your Mom and as well as Charlotte. Get it? We can't do it. The Chief has tied our hands, so it is up to you, Man," Preston almost orders Rob with concern in this voice.

Back at his parent's house, Rob wanders out to "Bob's Think Tank" and sits in her chair, waiting. Rob knows this is where Bob does her work and her thinking, "whatever she does." As he sits, trying to understand his mom, Preston's words run through his mind.

Finally, Rob goes back into the house and explains to Charlotte that whatever it takes, and from whomever they have to borrow, they have to bail Bob out of jail. Charlotte suggests they call Jane's mother, Alice. "Wow, what a great idea!" Rob is honestly surprised Charlotte came up with a descent thought.

Rob calls Alice. Alice calls other neighbors, including Grace, the nurse. Soon a rather large assemblage of friends, neighbors, and acquaintances whose lives Bob has touched, largely through the annual Easter Egg party show up at the front door, each with as much as they can afford to contribute to the "Bob Ebner Release Fund."

The entire family is amazed.

As Bob is led out of the holding cell, she sees Rob and Charlotte. "You crazy kids, what did you have to sell to get me out?" asks Bob. "Nothing, Mom, honest this is all from your friends. I never knew you had so many. Geez, all I did was call Alice," remarks Rob. "Yeah, and that was my idea," Charlotte chimes in. With a big smile on her face, Bob says, "Hmmm, I guess it is true that what goes around comes around. Come on. Let's get out of here." She grabs both kids around their wastes and says, "Any money left?" Rob nods. "We just have to use it to save that "Funny Water Spring." Yes, that is what I am calling it," Bob states emphatically.

42.

Radio DJ

One of Bob's neighbors and good friends are the local radio D.J., Ken Smith, and his wife, Bonnie. Every year they help at the Easter party. Ken serves is the DJ that oversees the egg hunt and prizes. They know and trust Bob. Both of them help the Ebner family hide the eggs and Bonnie Smith often helps underwrite the some of the costs.

Until after the shoot-out, Ken's job had kept him becoming involved, publicly. Now it is a news item. The public is in an uproar that two young people from their fair community could possible be the victims of a kidnap and even more angry about the total lack of support and respect from the Police Chief. Ken, risks his radio station but remembers what the water did for the little girl with the burns. His comments insight listeners to agree that it is the Chief, along with the kidnappers, who should be tried and not Bob.

According to Ken, Bob should be treated as a hero for saving her son and girlfriend rather being arrested. He goes "on the air" with his comments and drives his point. His arguments, and those of his faithful callers, sway many of the police officers into helping, so long as they can do it on the "q.t." Speculation grows that the Chief's actions are borne from a personal vendetta. His unrequited love for Bob's older sister, Angle Summit, is finally being avenged. Of course Ken gently persuades and encourages his listeners to believe that argument, whether it is true or not, and Ken honestly maintains that it is possible. Soon other listeners begin to agree and are outraged that the Chief would or could allow personal feelings to interfere with his duties to the city.

The town people are reminded of the Easter parties and the real love and friendship that the Ebner's give freely.

Just about that time Angle stops by radio station, WWYW, and asks Ken if she can make a statement, for the Police Chief's benefit, hoping he will be listening.

Ken assists Angel in placing a pair of headphones on her head and placing the microphone close enough to amplify her voice, but not so close as to cause feedback. "Are you all set?" asks Ken. Angel nods. The assistant in the control booth holds up fingers, five, four, three, two and one.

"Good Afternoon, this is the Ken Smith Show coming to you on WWYW, Vallivue Falls. We have been discussing the frightening kidnapping that occurred right here in our beautiful community. Some of you have called in suggesting stating that you have known the Chief of Police since he was a little tyke and many more of you remember him from his glory days in high school. It has even been suggested that his recent actions or should we say, lack thereof, in providing safety to the Ebner family is a result of his love interest in the oldest daughter, Angel Ebner

Summit. Well, Ladies and Gentlemen, this afternoon in our very own radio station, we have a treat for you.

Good afternoon, Mrs. Summit. May I call you Angel."

"Yes, that would be fine," replied Angel.

"And, might I say, you truly are. Ladies and Gentlemen, if you do not know this lovely young lady, let me just say that she is aptly named. . . truly heaven on Earth. I can see why the Chief fell in love with you," continues Ken.

Angel blushes.

"Forgive me. Listeners, I have known this young woman for many, many years. Her younger sister, Bob, the mother of one of the kids who were kidnapped, and I are neighbors and, more than neighbors, we have been friends for a long time. Isn't that right, Angel?"

Angel answers, "Yes. Let me just say, oh, gosh I am so nervous."

"There is nothing to be nervous about here. We are on your side, aren't we listeners? If you agree that we are on Angel's side, let me see you light up that call board," requests Ken.

Suddenly every little light on the board begins to blink. "See?"

Angel nods and continues, "I just want to speak to the Chief and remind him about the days when the three of us would do things together. Remember Todd? Remember when we were all in college? You two were best buds. The three of us were best buddies. I have always loved you. You are a terrific guy. It is only that," as the tone of her voice seems to change as if she still has feelings for the chief, "I fell in love with Todd. But, that has been a long time ago," she continues wistfully. "If you ever truly have loved me once, and I was not just an acquisition between rivaling playmates, then please, I beg you, release my sister and help catch the rest of the gang. We need you. I need you."

"Anything else?" Ken asks.

"No," responds Angel. "Oh, only please Listeners, is that what you call them? Understand that the Chief of Police is really a nice guy – at least the Chief I know. Give him a chance. Let's all work together on this. Thank you, Ken."

Angel gets up from the chair and shakes Ken's hand to walk out of building. "Just a moment, Angel, I'll walk out with you. My spot is over for the day," Ken says in a sort of fatherly manner. As the walk towards the exit of the radio station, Big Mommy walks in. This really shocks Ken Smith.

"You that Ken Smith guy?" Big Momma asks abruptly. Ken nods his head yes. "I'm gonna make a statement, but only with you," she continues.

Ken looks at Angel and shrugs his shoulders as if to ask her what else could he do. Bob Momma is insistent. Angel tells him to go on as Ken stands speechless for a moment, staring and studying Big Mommas' face. Then he suddenly remembers her from many Easter parties. She always has a friendly attitude and is truly giving to all the children.

Ken smiles and says, "Come on into studio A." This is not his normal time slot so he takes the mike from one of the other DJ's and says, "This is Ken Smith breaking in this afternoon show to bring you a special announcement." He hands the mike to Aunt Helen who says, "This is Aunt Helen from Big Momma's restaurant. It's time for all of us to get together and help, Roberta Ebner, you know her as Bob. She needs your help and she needs it now!" She hands the mike back and Ken who pauses and says, "You've now heard it from Big Momma, Bob's sister Angle Summit and Ken Smith at " WWYW," 1401 FM Radio. Now back to your regular show."

As they walk out of the studio Ken says to Big Momma, "Aunt Helen, I'm always doing the announcing at the

Easter party so we really don't get to work together, but I always watch you. You work up a real sweat with the kids and gifts and never seem to ask for anything in return." He stops in the hall and turns to her and says, "Anything you need or that I can do for you, just call, period, just call. Now how about that hug you so richly deserve? You've got such a big heart. Let me spread a little sugar your way," Ken says with a softness in his voice and gleam in his eye as he gives her one huge bear hug. The total admiration for each other is evident as Aunt Helen hugs Ken back. With an unusual lightness in her step for such a large person, she walks out.

43.

Built Steel Hut

Thanks to her neighbors, friends and family, Bob is out of jail on bail. She sells enough water to Ken, who has always been on her side to build a steel hut to protect her and Rob at the spring.   Rob, now that he understands what his mom has been through, decides to accompany her on her next trip.

First, they go to "Jack's Fab Shop," a medium size steel fabricating shop.   Like most people in Vallivue, he is a friend. Together they design a sort of safe-house for the spring connecting directly onto a trailer.

Not much bigger than the old style phone booth, it has two layers of steel.   The inner wall is stainless steel for safety with various hangers for guns, rifles, water, oxygen, first aid kit and more.   Almost imperceptible holes are built into the walls for adequate ventilation and looking out.

The welded steel hut lays on its side as part of the trailer. To set it up at the spring, all they have to do is stand it up on its tail end into a foundation.

Bob and Rob load up the Bronco for the trip for the four of them including, Barney and Betty in the back seat. Barney and Betty aren't sure about this trip because they can't see out the windshield. They trust Rob to 'ride shot gun," but only after conferring with each other and even then, somewhat reluctantly.

Bob makes her normal stop at the gas station at the edge of town. In lieu of comments from the spineless guys who laughed at Bob on her first trip they cheer her and Rob. Several of them help load everything Bob and Rob bought. They all come out and send them off with old high school football chants, some of them bringing last minute care packages of things Bob and Rob would not have considered including, but might come in handy. The station manager turns up the loud speakers to the tune, "You've Got What It Take."

The long trip is so uneventful that Rob falls asleep for a short while, at least until Bob starts down the winding road with all the washed out ruts and bounces Rob's head into the door window. He jumps up and wants to fight the ugly thugs who kidnapped him and Charlotte. After coming to his senses he sees his mom. Bob smiles and says, "Welcome to the valley! This next part of the ride is rough. When we get down to the bottom of this road, we drive back through the trees to the spring. Then you'll get to see the prettiest little valley: so peaceful and quiet." Bob takes a deep breath and sighs. Rob, hearing a change in her voice, looks over and sees a equal change in her eyes and says, "Mom, I'm sorry for not believing you for the last few months. These last few days have gone so fast with the kidnapping, virus, hospital, Charlotte being pregnant and the Funny Water and, oh yeah, you being in jail. I don't know where to start to sort it all out and make any sense of it."

Bob slows the Bronco down to a creep, grabs Rob's arm and says, "You and Charlotte are going to be parents soon and then you will understand the how's and why's parents do things for their families and friends. There are no simple answers to some of things that we do, but your dad and I are proud of you and Berta. Yes, even Berta, because she's still young and learning in her own way, just as you did."

They both sit in silence for the ride down the ruts and to the bridge. Then Bob stops and gets out to lock in the hubs on the driver's side as Rob hops out and locks in the hubs on the passenger's side.

As they ride through the trees and bushes to the clearing and the valley, Rob's eyes open wide. He stands on the running board of the Bronco and looks out over this paradise exclaiming, "Wow!" The sound reverberates down the valley sending a slight echo.

Bob takes Rob on a tour of the spring and campsite area. She has already worked out where to set up everything in her mind. Bob has Rob back the trailer into a spot near the spring and unhook the trailer, trailer lights and hitch.

Bob and Rob dig a pit for the hut, pour some dry concrete mix in the hole, dump a few buckets of water in with the concrete and tilt the trailer/hut up on its back end. Once they check the sides with a level and back fill dirt around the lower part of the hut to make it sit straight, the hut is good to go.

Next, they build safety devices at the spring . At first Rob is all thumbs, but Bob is very patient with him and would rather talk him through it so he could gain a sense of accomplishment than to build and set the devices herself, even though this process takes longer. Bob is beaming with pride that Rob is taking an interest. In the scheme of things, time is of little moment to her. Along with the safe house they set explosives all the way around the spring area including over the Funny Water Spring. This will destroy the spring but may save their lives.

She leaves two notes for Ed. Even though she has never seen him see feels so intently that there is a friend out there who has been a kind of guardian angel, particularly that first night when she made so many trips to the outhouse. She does not want him hurt. One of the notes reads,

Dear Ed:

My son is with me this time

and he may be back for me.

We may have been followed

by some mob guys who tried

to kill my son and his girlfriend.

Be careful. They have guns.

We placed safety devices all over

to help save us if they show up.

Be careful my friend. Don't get hurt.

I hope to see you someday.

Bob

The other note indicates where the explosives have been set, including those around the Funny Water Spring.

After a few days of camping and filling as many bottles as they brought with them, they load up and head for home. When they return R.C., Berta and Charlotte are all waiting for them at home with open arms. To Bob and Rob it feels almost back to normal, if it not for the Funny Water and the many questions.

Bob realizes that with everything going on in her life, including her many trips, she feels the urgency to speak with someone who can console her spirit. She talks to the Pastor of her church. He provides her with inspirational passages which she promptly hangs on the think tank walls. One handwritten note reminds Bob of the virtues of the water in lieu of personal riches.

44.

Government Agency

Max Katz from R.C.'s law firm calls Bob, without R.C. knowing. He gives her guidance on how to get in touch with a particular government agency and have the site checked out by the USA satellite system.

Bob makes the calls and commissions a government agency to take satellite pictures and infrared color images of the area to see if there are any other places on Earth that show the same images. To do this, she uses every bit of available credit on her credit cards and hopes she can sell enough water to pay the cards off before R.C. finds out.

In some hidden room at some secretive locale, a government nerd, Weldon, or Wel as his friends call him, who has been given this project from his boss, plays with the government satellite computer. Something about the tone in his voice when his boss gave him this project set the Weldon's nerves on end. He has always been a nerd and through the years has developed a kind of Sixth Sense when presented with a project he knows his supervisor sees as frivolous. It is something about the snide tone or crooked smile that almost implies, "Here you go, Kid. This is another dumb one. We don't expect you to succeed with it, but we hope it will confound you long enough to keep you out of hair for a while."

Usually, when presented with a project like this one, it is the supervisor who actually lacks sufficient sophistication to see the true beauty and value to the work, but the Weldon knows. Even his name is somehow prophetic in the well of knowledge required to solve some of the puzzles that have absolutely eluded others never seems to reach bottom. Still, he has long learned in instances like this that he must protect himself and so he changes a few computer settings. As he sets up the program, he adds a memory system for the government report to read negative reports and diverts the real findings to an unknown computer.

45.

The FBI

All this information is being gathered and analyzed by the FBI who send agents to investigate, knowing the local police are staying out of the picture except to observe.

As a complete surprise, agents show up at the house and take Bob, R.C., Charlotte and Berta to a schoolyard just a few blocks away. Their instructions are to keep them safe and away from their home until the Section Chief arrives.

In a private government jet, still hundreds of miles away, a man sits in a very comfortable airplane seat with four reports on the table before him. Reading the reports, in total disgust, he promptly gets on the phone. The man in the plane is known as "J. R.," a very high ranking FBI agent whose reputation is well known around the agency. He is a strictly "by the book" short of man, but "his book" in that he is self-made and sometimes the two books conflict. His always wins.

As he reads the reports he telephones Brig. Gen. Myrna Williams. She sits at her desk in the Pentagon. Their conversation begins as if the two of them were very good friends. In fact, the verbal jousting between the two of them implies that at one time they may have been more than friends. Parts of the conversation, in double intenders, is rarely heard between members of the opposite sex unless they were once lovers. Still, there is a very professional edge to the tone of their voices.

J.R. gets to the point and asks the General for some serious help, stressing the word "serious" so he is certain she knows what he is talking about. He explains that he is on his way to Vallivue Falls airport to clear up the mess at Bob's. He requests Huey helicopters for transportation to the spring and an Apache gun ship from the military, but cannot go through regular channels. For one thing, it would take too long. For another, although the FBI does not engage in black ops, until he can fully investigate the situation, he does not need the headache of interagency squabbling. "Let's just say that it is a kidnapping issue," he reasons to the General. "Can you arrange for two Hueys and an Apache from a local National Guard unit? I really don't care to go through the governor since there is a possible issue of misconduct on the part of the local police. My research indicates there is a Guard unit on its last week of an exercise only forty-five miles from the site," he suggests. "It will cost you dinner at a restaurant of my choosing, theatre at the Kennedy Center in D.C. and a night of dancing," she jokingly bargains. J. R. loves the blackmail. The thought of dinner, theatre and dancing with the very attractive female general makes J.R. smile, but he has to get back to the reports before his plane lands. "The price certainly is within my budget. Thank you, Sir, always a pleasure," he teases her.

As he hangs up the phone, J.R. reclines in his chair for what seems like just a moment daydreaming about the general and the last time he was with her. "Damn, why did I ever let her go?" he thinks to himself as his eyes close. He wakes up just as the plane lands and chides himself for having not finished reading the reports.

On the tarmac, Huey, Eagle #614 is waiting for him. He finishes reading the reports in Eagle #614 and has them in his hand, securely as he steps out of the helicopter. The landing site is at the Middle school play ground near Bob's house.

In the distance Bob answers her cell phone. It is Rob. He is defending himself from the steel bunker he and Bob built. Just as J. R. suspected the "gang" has attacked the Spring. "There must be twenty of them," he reports to Bob in a seemingly calm voice. Only he and Bob know what they have in store outside the bunker for any trespassers.

Two of the agents approach J.R. to discuss the situation, but he has no time for that and promptly brings up the reports he's been reading, making it clear that two of the reports look like chapters from "War and Peace." Two other reports are condensed versions of only three pages each, including a cover page. They seem to have the same information and he didn't fall asleep reading them.

The pitfall of relying on condensed versions of anything is that you place your trust in some individual, who you don't know, to have sufficient experience and knowledge of any situation to determine what is and what is not important. Too many times he witnessed agents, and good ones, rely only on the condensed reports only to their ultimate failure in a mission. Still, no one has time to read novellas and in his experience, agents who describe in detail are often caught in the tree limbs rather than seeing the forest.

The truly gifted agent knows how to tell the truth with sufficient detail to make it plausible. Anything more is too much and that is one distinction between a good agent and a gifted agent.

Two agents are promptly sent to the school front lawn and parking lot to guard the FBI cars and the bicycle rack before the grade school students are released from class. At the same time, they are charged with re-writing their reports into a condensed version.

The other two agents are told to stay close by and to brief and organize the other fully armed agents, who just arrived, in the current situation. "Get ready to load but under no circumstances, and I repeat, under NO circumstances are you to engage until so ordered.

As J. R. and Bob talk, they head for the first Huey with R.C. The second Huey (Eagle #283) will take Charlotte and Berta.

Berta seems attracted to a rookie agent. She maneuvers herself to be able to ride next to him. The attraction seems mutual. As they are boarding, Apache #409 arrives overhead.

The two agents who submitted the good reports understand J. R.'s methods and are happy to be working with him. Agent Dexter has worked with J. R. before and tells agent Tucker not to be so nervous, that J.R. is by the book that he wrote and does not care what color or religion he is so long as the agent is a full team player. Just then J.R. puts Tucker in the seat on the other side of Bob. Tucker look bewildered. He is unsure as to why. J.R. catches that ill-feeling and tells Tucker that he has worked with Dexter before and after seeing Tucker's report, he feels Tucker will be a good right hand man for the day. Dexter gives Tucker a thumbs up signifying, "see I told you so." Tucker sits up straighter with his chin held high.

J. R. turns to Bob and wants the design and lay-out of the spring area and commands Agents Tucker and Dexter to put on headsets to listen.

46.

Nerd

Back in Washington, D.C., Weldon, the nerd, is finally able to get a good reading on the spring from the satellite. Normally it takes about eight hours to get a clear image of the spring and its location, or any specific relatively small location. Even at that, some images are more clear than others, largely depending upon the weather pattern and topology of the location. If the images are not sufficient Weldon knows he will have to search for other locations that are close, geographically, for a good read. Time is clearly of the essence

At the same time Weldon is secretly transferring classified information to an unknown off-sight computer. Although Wel has secured the information necessary to locate Bob's mountain, spring, and ultimately her campsite, he has seen to it that the relevant information is diverted immediately to the off-site computer with no trace to the office one. He simply does not trust his boss and, in this instance, is even more circumspect. Very carefully, Weldon disguises his actions as he continues to download to the work computer and download to the off-site computer information based on the two different parameters he constructed.

He has programmed his Government computer to show only false negative reports for this project.   No matter what comes through the system it will show distorted images and infrared color images that will not match anything. Simultaneously, transfers the real information automatically to his computer at home.

The images of the Spring have to remain steady for eight minutes every time the satellite passes overhead for the next four to eight revolutions around the Earth and the transference of data must appear seamless.

47.

At The Spring

Rob is in the steel hut, which is being surrounded by what looks like twenty armed men with, of all people, Big Al who is hidden from Rob's line of sight. Rob telephones Bob, "Mom, I think we are really in for it. There must be twenty or twenty-five men here. What is your situation?"

Rob runs out of time as the men move closer to the hut, "It's too late. I have to blow the spring," Rob says to Bob.

"Are you certain there is no alternative?" Bob asks with a note of sadness in her voice.

"Yeah. You know those guys who kidnapped me and Charlotte? Well, I'm pretty sure I recognize the voices of some of them. They are up to no good and, from what you told me and what I have experienced of that funny water from the spring, we can't let it get in their hands," Rob reasons.

"No, no, of course you are right. Do what you have to do," Bob replies.

Rob cannot hear the Apache gun ship arrive as he blows up the spring and its surroundings so no one will misuse the powers of the "Funny Water."

48.

Rescue

As the Apache gun ship, AH-409, flies down through the valley headed for the spring area, the pilot sees a large cloud of smoke, dust and dirt fly up into the air over the spring.

The pilot carefully maneuvers to the east around the smoke and over the stream to gain a better view of the campsite and Spring area. His rotor washes over the area clearing enough smoke for a better view of ten staggering bodies coughing and wiping their eyes as they attempt to crawl out from under the dirt and limbs from the explosion. He switches on his loudspeaker and makes the announcement, "Stay where you are. Do not attempt to leave the area. This is Major Lewis of Apache 409. Our guns are trained on your position." Major Lewis has aimed the 30 mm nose gun down at the camp but has not flipped the switch to arm it.

Big Al's minions stand still, shocked with the noise of the explosion and can only hear and see enough to get the idea that moving is not in their best interest.

Just then Eagle #614 arrives and Apache 409 rises straight up moving north over the stream to allow J. R. and the Huey to land. Armed agents deploy and survey the area. J. R. exits, but has Bob and the others held back until all is clear.

The hut, no longer erect, lies on its side. J. R.'s vision is hampered by the dirt covering the steel hut. No sign of life is visible to him even though his Intel suggests fourteen thugs/terrorists, including Big Al, arrived at the spring.

The pilot for Eagle #283 sees a spot just east, about 100 yards, and lands. More armed agents deploy on the spring side of the stream. As they quickly head for the spring area, J. R. is on his headset telling them to look for anyone moving or hiding. Two agents stay with the Huey: one for protecting it and the other for protecting the passengers. The young rookie agent who first seemed to pay special attention to Berta is the agent left behind to protect the passengers.

Back at the spring, the agents round up the ugly thugs with little or no resistance. "Never overestimate the stupidity of your adversary," J.R. says with a wry smile on his face.

"Did the government satellite system have enough time?" he wonders, half out loud.

Bob exits the Huey as the thugs are led toward the helicopter. "Why don't you rest a bit?" J.R. asks her noticing how drawn her face had become from complete fatigue. The terrorists/thugs are pushed into a huddle behind the Huey, guarded by agents.

"You three over there come with me," J.R. commands three agents. "We have to get to the steel bunker." Looking toward Bob and making certain that she is out of earshot, he looks to his agents and says, "The more time has elapsed, the less likely we are to find survivors."

The steel safety bunker that Bob, Rob and Jack, the welder, built has been blown over with Rob inside. From a quick survey of the situation, it appears that it is half covered up with dirt. At least the frame is readily visible. That is a good thing.

Although Bob had not heard J.R. speaking to his agents about the bunker and survivors, she had read his lips. "Silly man," she thought. "When are they going to learn that not all women are alike. Humph, and they are supposed to be the stronger sex."

Bob takes a deep breath and pushes aside the feelings that this situation should be different because it is her son. She loudly and methodically knocks on the bunker allowing time between raps to call out to Rob. From inside the bunker, Rob listens to his Mom's voice and slowly moves his head slightly so that the oxygen mask through which he has been breathing is moved slightly to the side allowing him to continue to receive oxygen and still, in a somewhat muffled voice, returns Bob's calls. "I'm okay, Mom. I'm okay."

Agents clear the dirt away and set the bunker back upright. Rob opens the door. Oxygen tanks somehow managed to remain strapped to one wall. The Dasani water bottles did not fair as well and are all over the place. "Amazing what remains intact, huh?" Rob asks Bob with relief in his voice. His rifle hanging on the wall and pistol in his holster appear as if the bunker had suffered no more than the slamming of the door. The room has peep holes and small windows on all sides with covers. "Now do you see why we had all of these holes, Rob?

Made breathing just a bit easier, didn't it?" Bob asks Rob. "Really couldn't say, Mom. I had my trusty mask," Rob teases Bob and gives one of the agents a "high five" as he walks by overhearing the conversation. "Oh, you just come here. You are going to get the biggest hug you have had in years." Bob jumps up and down and hugs Rob.

Suddenly someone begins to cough and groan from a pile just six feet away. One agent sees a corner of Rob's dirt covered tent move and jerks it off revealing another Ugly who can't see or hear and has no idea what just happened.

Bob, Rob and the Agent look at each other, take a deep breath of relief and laugh as the agents directs him to the other thugs.

From across the stream a load bellowing voice yells out, "Bob!" As the agents train their rifles on the far side they see one ugly fly out of the bushes into the water and then another. Then a large bearded man emerges from the brush holding the Big Al, the little runt, by the collar. He stretches his arm out over the edge of a rock high above the water.

J. R. quickly pushes the button on his headset and in his commanding voice says, "Train your weapons on the little runt. "If he gets wet, don't let him get away. "Some of you other guys pick up the ones already in the water."

Bob holds her hand up in the air and calls to the one she thinks might be her "Ed," "Is that you?" Ed drops the little one off the rock and puts his right hand up in the air to wave to Bob in return. J.R. hits his button again and says, "Get that little S.O.B. in the water." As the agents get the little guy the big mountain man disappears into the woods. J. R. watches Ed and just smiles to himself.

One of the agents quickly pushes his button and asks, "Sir, what about the big guy?" J.R. pauses and replies, "What big guy? I didn't see any big guy? Did you? Take a moment and think real hard. Did you see a big guy? Are you absolutely certain, without any doubt that you saw a BIG guy? All I saw was that the little S.O.B. just slipped on the rock and fell into the water. Isn't that exactly what you saw, Agent?"

Bob looks at J.R. and is speechless. J.R. has already figured out who this mystery man is and that the Bob's "Ed" was a good friend and protector of Bob. Only Bob can hear J.R. say, "Gotta watch for that darn slippery rock," in such a manner that Bob isn't certain if J.R. was referring to a wet rock or nominating her "friend," Ed.

Dexter looks at Tucker and Tucker gives him the thumbs-up. All the agents and passengers from Eagle #283 arrive through the trees and brush. Berta runs over to give her brother an unexpected big hug, as Bob looks on and thinks to herself, "Maybe Berta is proud of her big brother and will come around, after all." Berta looks at Bob as if she had read Bob's mind and smiles, mouthing the words, "I love you."

Some agents react like a football team that just scored the winning touchdown. Other agents not assigned to guard the dirty, dusty gang turn to Bob and Rob and ask what needs to be cleaned up.

J.R. radios the Apache gun ship. Bob touches his arm to get his attention asking, "May I hug you?" He looks into her eyes, and says, "Yes, Ma'am, as long as the men don't think I make a habit of it." "Thank you," she whispers into his ear and places a soft kiss on his check, "Thank you very much." J.R., in his stout way, almost shows tears in his eyes.

The AH-409 heads east out of the valley on its way back to base as the clean up continues. Bob and Rob supervise the spring area. Gold plates are loaded into Eagle #614. Eagle #283 is loaded with Berta and her "special" agent escort, Bryan Best, along with everyone except Bob, R.C., Rob, Char and J.R. who stay with the gold.

Eagle #614 takes off first just after Bob writes a note to Ed and throws it across the stream for him to read later. Some of the agents, intrigued, watch Bob and attempt to look over her shoulder to see what she is writing. J.R. moves in behind her, between Bob's back and the agents, looks at them and with a swirling gesture of his hand indicates that they should look the other way and continue the clean up.

As they take off in the helicopter, Bob sees Ed out of the corner of her eye, holding the note and rock up. A smile of relief crosses Bob's face. J. R. also sees Ed and just a small curl of a smile runs up one corner of his mouth.

49.

Claim

As soon as Bob and R.C. return to town, Bob researches ownership and mining rights of the area in the county library. It is a slow process pouring through voluminous documents in the books and many of the pages are brittle with age. "R.C., it seems that no one owns the land around the Spring," Bob whispers to R.C. "No kidding? Are you sure?" R.C. responds. "Yeah, look at this," Bob points to the map that clearly indicates the Spring but there are no roadways into it. "The plat maps do not seem to have changed since they were first surveyed in the early 1920's," Bob again whispers in amazement.

Bob and R.C. approach the County Clerk and ask for the Homestead Claim and Claim of Mineral Rights. As they fill out the paperwork, R.C. is still amazed. "You are really certain?" he asks. "Pretty sure. Let's fill out the paperwork here and see what the Clerk says. If someone else has an ownership interest, it should be in their system."

"That will be $40.00," says the Clerk as she stamps their claims. Bob and R.C. filed a mining claim and homestead claim on the gold and land surrounding the Spring. "Now you can study the "funny water" to your little heart's content," R.C. chides Bob. Bob smiles, then suddenly feels a pit in her stomach. What about Ed?

50.

Months Later At Easter

Many months have passed. Once again, the Ebner family stands at the church entrance waiting for Rob and Charlotte to arrive for Easter service. This time there are three of them. Charlotte and Rob are the proud parents of a son whose Baptismal is today

R. C. and Bob wait in on a beautiful grassy knoll, seemingly in a circle, with Alice, her husband and three other couples. All reminisce about the past year, how fast it went and how some things never change. As always, Rob and Charlotte are late for church. "I suppose that is a sign that everything is back to normal," R.C. quips as he looks at his watch. Everyone laughs. "Yes indeedy, some things just never change," Alice's husband offers.

J.R., the FBI Director, and his new wife General Myrna arrive with agents Dexter, Tucker and the young Bryan Best. As Agent Best approaches the family, Berta walks from behind the bushes where she once hid with her friends.

In the past year there has been an amazing transformation in her: no more gothic attire, multiple piercings, and tattoos. This beautiful young lady, with long wavy hair, walks toward Best, puts her arms around him in a hug and says, "Hello, Agent Best," with a brilliant twinkle in her eyes. "Hello!" Agent Best responds kissing her.

"You know being the Godparents of Bobbie we are responsible for the tyke growing up morally. Are we up to that?" he asks Berta. "I think I am. I know you are, after all, look at the wonderful influence you have on me. You do something to me," Berta begins in earnest then teases Best.

Secretly arriving is the mountain man "Ed" on his chrome and black Harley to wish them all well. He shaved his beard and dressed like the man pictured with his wife and sons on the mantel of his fireplace in the mountains.

J.R. knows the mountain man, walks up to him and says, "Ah, Mr. Foster, we finally get to meet." The mountain man, certain that no would recognize him, is immediately taken aback, but quickly regains his composure that is so much of his training. Without a word, he starts to turn toward his bike. Agents Dexter and Tucker are just behind and step in his way.

Bob sees all of this and is shocked until it dawns on her that J.R. must know this man and that he must be her "Ed." At least he resembles the photograph she saw on his mantel so many months ago. She starts walking quickly over to them. "Darn heals," she says out loud as her shoes sink into the damp lawn.

J.R. tells "Ed," whose first name happens to be Edward, "Ed, I've got some good news and some bad news." People stand still and conversations go silent like an E. F. Hutton commercial on television as their ears all seem to turn towards J.R. and this big guy, Ed, standing in front of him. Even Bob, who has moved closer to the two and is now standing beside Angel stops in her tracks. Angel and Police Chief Jason Rugger, standing arm and arm, are too speechless to acknowledge Bob with more than a smile.

"The good news is that your past has been expunged by an attorney that owed me a favor. You're free to go, almost. The kidnappers at the mountain shoot out all had warrants and rewards on their heads, so I had the attorney, establish a reward and accept it in your name. J.R. reaches for something inside his suit coat. Bob gasps. Not knowing what he is doing and fearing the worst. J.R. hearing Bob, slowly pulls his right hand holding an envelope in it and hands it to Ed Foster. Ed opens the envelope and reads the check made out to him in a sizable amount.

J.R. then shows Ed a motor home being driven in front of the church and says, "See that motor home? Quite a beauty, isn't she?" J.R. asks Ed as the vehicle comes to a stop.

Ed, looking inside the front window, sees a beautiful lady from the picture on his fireplace hearth in the mountains. Ed looks to J.R., not certain if the "Quite a beauty" comment referred to the motor home or the driver. He looks back to the motor home. His two sons, all in smiles, wave to him from the opened back windows. "Well, what are you waiting for," J.R. questions Ed as he gives him a shove, "Go! That is an order, Sir!" Agents Dexter and Tucker give each other a thumbs-up. J. R. catches it and smiles.

Bob is still standing, speechless. Chief Rugger speaks up and asks J.R., "What's the bad news?"

J. R. turns and says, chuckling, "I don't know. It just sounded good." And many close by break out in laughter

Bob notices that J.R. still seems a bit edgy, like he was waiting for someone else or something else. "Let's all get into the church and get this baby Baptized," she says, trying to herd everyone indoors.

J.R. secretly is waiting for Weldon, who is expected to show up at any moment. J.R. has been tracking him for a month after he left the government satellite job he had for eighteen years rather abruptly and with a spurious explanation.

After most of the Congregation are in the church, Weldon arrives in his old Ford Pinto. Even though it is a relic, the car is in mint condition.

J.R. waits just inside the church door, hidden from Weldon's view as he creeps into the church and looks around holding a small picture in his hand. The photograph is a computer-generated picture of Bob's driver's license: not a particularly flattering photograph. J.R. gives Agents Dexter and Tucker hand signals instructing them to watch him.

J.R. walks along the side of the vestibule, nicknamed the "groom's walk," leading just in front of and slightly to the side of the alter. His wife, Myrna, Angel and Chief Rugger are seated in the pew just behind Bob, R.C., Berta and her new husband, Agent Best. Rob and Charlotte are seated in the pew ahead of them with baby Robert, III, in Charlotte's arms.

The minister motions for Rob and Charlotte to come forward and inquires of the Congregation, "Who will stand for this child?" Berta and Bryan rise to join the Minister answering, "We do."

Just then, J. R. notices the Weldon slowly, silently, creeping to where Bob is standing. He startles Bob as he introduces himself and, stuttering, tries to explain to Bob that he was the government satellite computer controller when she hired them to search for satellite color images and other sites like hers in California. He apologizes for scaring her.

J.R. sits and leans forward in the pew, his hand ready on his pistol just in case it is needed, to hear the nerd tell Bob of the real results he's been studying for the past year. Bob wonders why this creepy guy would care? He states his old boss would have kept the secrets for himself and "He's mean, too, so I quit."

Bob quickly glances at J.R. for reassurance convinced that the nerd is less than hard wired properly. J.R. winks as if to say, "I've got your back side. No need to worry."

Weldon begins to explain that he has found locations of three places on Earth with the same satellite readings: one just 400 yards from the original one; one in Switzerland; and one in Australia.

Bob, unable to contain herself with the joy of hearing this good news, remarks, "YES! YES! YES! I knew I was right."

Rob and Charlotte have a bewildered look on their faces and as they are about to say something Bob looks up and sees everyone staring at her. She realizes she has made quite a scene.

Although her thoughts run wild with the idea what she can do and add so much joy to the world, she sheepishly looks around and says, "Sorry." To the Minister, she says, "You can go on now."

"Well, thank you. Ladies and gentlemen, we have been blessed with the grandmother's permission. God will be pleased," the Minister responds, to which the Congregation is hard pressed to keep from laughing.

Bob and R.C move over enough for Weldon to sit beside them as J.R, Myrna, Angle and the Chief lean forward to hear more.

During the Baptism, Rob pulls tattered papers from Bob's think tank wall and reads the poem, "If" and officially names their son, Robert Charles Ebner, III.

Tears run down Bob's face as Rob finishes. R.C. puts his head down so the tears welling in his eyes are not visible and even J.R. coughs.

All cheer for Robert, III, and for what ever has made Bob extremely happy. They seem to sense it has something to do with the Funny Water.

Berta, Bryan, Rob, Charlotte and little Rob return to their seats in the front row for the closing moments of the service. The Minister makes the final remark that this year's Easter Egg Hunt at the Ebner's has been moved to the park. "We have much to praise God for this year. Now go and have some fun," the Minister closes.

Outside of the church there is a great deal of commotion and unanswered questions as children tug at their parents' clothing wanting to be the first to get to the party.

51.

Easter Egg Hunt

This year the annual "Easter Egg Hunt and Party" is being held in a nearby park. With the aid of the money from the gold, R.C. and Bob have rented it for the day. The park has all of the play equipment, baseball diamond, football field and catering facilities needed.

Berta is still in charge of hiding the eggs. With so many to hide she has enlisted the usual candidates, other mom's and her friends, who finally grew up. Only this year, Agent Best joins in the fun of hiding the eggs, occasionally catching a glimpse of his beautiful and pregnant wife, Berta.

She runs up to him and says, "Next year you will be a daddy. Are you nervous about that?" "Me? Nervous?" Bryan's voice quivers as he holds Berta in his arms and gently rubs her ever so slightly showing tummy. "Yes, absolutely."

Chuck, the ice cream man, pulls his truck into place with the music blaring trying to keep the attention of the little ones so they do not notice precisely where the eggs are being hidden.

"Absolutely," Bryan repeats. "But, as someone quite wise told me, very recently, I might add, I think I am ready. I know you are, after all, look at the wonderful influence you have on me. You do something to me – something that simply mystifies me."

Slightly over a small hill and under trees is a perfect area for the elderly and little babies. What the boughs are unable to shade, tents do. Food items are in some tents nearby and that's Big Momma's department with all of her staff enjoying everything and everyone. Tiny is too busy with eight kids at the egg hunt for Big Momma to bother him.

Radio station "WWYW," again provides a live remote broadcast with five announcers helping Ken Smith and his wife, Bonnie who also brings a truck load of presents for the egg winners. Ken and Bonnie watch carefully to make certain every child receives a present.

The airport shuttle bus owner is there. Drivers driving golf carts help the elderly and anyone who seems to be able to use assistance. When he isn't busy, he spends time at the grills. His buddy with the portable potties has them in the right spot for everyone. In an enclosed area, covered with screens, wigs and parts of costumes fly as impersonators don their attire and prepare their make-up. A passerby who listens carefully can hear throats clearing and scales sung as the impersonators practice their affectations.

52.

OH, What An End

(and A Beginning)

Ed and his family join in the festivities. Bob approaches them and offers Ed a job as the mining superintendent for all the locations. "You understand," Bob asks to Ed, his wife, and the two children with a twinkle in her eyes, "that you will have to travel with him to check the various sites?" "Can we? Can we, really, Dad?" squeal the kids with excitement. "What about school?" asks Ed's wife. Ed looks at her with such warmth, excitement and appreciation and responds, "Darling, I believe between the two of us we have nearly a dozen degrees. I think we can handle home schooling." She sighs.

Next, Bob approaches the government nerd, Weldon Smaller. "Come with me," she says to Weldon, taking him by the hand, "There is someone I want you to meet. Betty Cutter, kind of a wallflower in terms of social skills, is standing all along continually pushing her glasses up on her nose as if the pair were too big for her. "Betty, it would please me to introduce to you my friend, Weldon Smaller, a true computer wizard. Weldon, I am honored to present to you Betty Cutter, the owner of "Bits and Bytes," the local computer store."

After a brief awkward moment, and a nudge from Bob, Betty begins to speak to Weldon. Bob quietly slips away but secretly checks in on them from time to time. They seem to really hit it off, just as Bob guessed they would. "Do you think you two could work together?" she asks. Betty and Weldon both look at each other and simultaneously blush. Without waiting for their response and seeing the look on their faces, Bob says, "Terrific! You two are my new location coordinators. I will need you to be in close communication with each other."

Finally, Bob approaches the retired FBI/newly married J.R. aside. "I love to save the best for last," Bob states as she puts an arm around J.R. and guides him in the direction of where Berta and Bryan are standing. "Now that you are no longer with the agency, I insist you serve as our Chief of Security. There is, however, one provision – that you accept soon to be ex-Agent Best, our Bryan, as your assistant."

J.R. looks at Bryan and says, "Son, one question, think back to the days when I had all of you writing reports, what was the longest report you submitted?

Bryan thinks for a moment. He knew those reports had been part of a test and was always uncertain whether he had passed or not. He remembered that the instructions included the direction to not sign the report or add any mark that would indicate its author. Certainly other agents seem to submit more complete reports. "Honestly, Sir," Bryan begins with trepidation, "Three pages."

"You're my man!" J.R. gleams as he grabs Bryan by the hand to give him a hardy shake, which turns into a hug. "Now don't you dare think I make a habit of that," J.R. concludes winking at Bob.

By this time all of the family has gathered around and caught up with Bob and after seeing this a major cheer goes up with all yelling "Happy Easter to all."

888888888888888888

JACK RISIN

The Author

I'm not sure how to describe myself, I started my first corporation at age 21 when the voting age was 21, it was the first Monday after I got married. My new bride had the courage and stamina to stay with me through the 60's, 70's, 80's and 90's until a doctor made a mistake and left me without my partner. This tragedy happened just six months before I had the opportunity to present this story as a treatment at a meeting of Directors, Producers, instructors and editor's of the movie industry.

In 1989 my biography was published for the first time by Marquis Publishing. Marquis has since expanded my biography in "Who's Who in the World," "Who's Who in America" and "Who's Who in Finance and Business." I owe a great deal to this publishing company for choosing me as a candidate for these books. Shortly after my name was published I was honored and asked to join a prestigious origination, "The International Platform Association." I describe this origination to others who want to know more about the members by simply telling them the list begins in 1831 with one of the founders, Daniel Webster, includes most of the U. S. presidents, Sir Winston Churchill, Bob Hope and then falls all the down to unworthy me.

My first annual conference was in 1993 where I met 800 members. It happened there. The first day a nice little elderly lady came up to me and asked what I did for a living. I proceeded to tell her I was a designer and manufacturer of large steel fabricated products. It seems she really wanted to listen to my voice. She than told me I should have my voice in the entertainment industry. Well I had heard that before, going all the ways back to high school, but growing up in rural Ohio that didn't seem to carry much weight. However, the next day the same happened and the third day again. I was getting a complex, mostly because of not understanding me. Also on the third day the Association introduced these fine ladies, all were retired actresses, producers and directors. I went back to my room and looked in the mirror and felt like slapping myself in an effort to wake-up.

I returned home and went to school again and became that actor. After attending the highly renowned 'Film Industry Workshop Inc' school of acting (known as FIWI) and doing the normal "extra" parts in some movies I worked hard and was chosen as a 'Stand-in', received my three union vouchers, joined SAG and did my craft in some great film productions.

The rest is present history.